Sherri L. King

An Ellora's Cave Romantica Publication

www.ellorascave.com

Bitten

ISBN 9781843604075

Cover Art by Darrel King.

This book printed in the U.S.A. by Jasmine-Jade Enterprises, LLC.

Electronic book Publication May 2004
Trade paperback Publication May 2004

Also by Sherri L. King

Bachelorette
Beyond Illusion
Caress of Flame
Ellora's Cavemen: Tales from the Temple III (*anthology*)
Ferocious
Fetish
Full Moon Xmas
Manaconda (*anthology*)
Midnight Desires (*with Kate Hill*)
Moon Lust 1: Moonlust
Moon Lust 2: Bitten
Moon Lust 3: Mating Season
Moon Lust 4: Feral Heat
Rayven's Awakening
Ride the Lightning
Sanctuary
Sin and Salvation
Sterling Files 1: Steele
Sterling Files 2: Vicious
Sterling Files 3: Fyre
Sterling Files 4: Hyde
The Horde Wars 1: Ravenous
The Horde Wars 2: Wanton Fire
The Horde Wars 3: Razors Edge
The Horde Wars 5: Lord of the Deep
The Jewel

About the Author

&

Sherri L. King lives in the American Deep South with her husband, artist and illustrator Darrell King. Critically acclaimed author of The Horde Wars and Moon Lust series, her primary interests lie in the world of action packed paranormals, though she's been known to dabble in several other genres as time permits.

Sherri welcomes comments from readers. You can find her website and email address on her author bio page at www.ellorascave.com.

Tell Us What You Think

We appreciate hearing reader opinions about our books. You can email us at Comments@EllorasCave.com.

BITTEN

Prologue

Ivan Basileus laid his hand over the firm roundness of his wife's very pregnant stomach. He growled low in his throat, a deep sound of satisfaction and contentment, as he felt his child nestled safely beneath his hand. Brianna, his wife and lifelong mate, smiled and placed her hand over his, entwining their fingers to strengthen the bond. He couldn't resist giving in to the lure of her nearness. He leaned in and kissed her fervently in the curve of her neck and shoulder, marveling anew at how lucky he was to have found the perfect match to his soul in her. He loved her so very much.

Brianna's breath caught audibly and her eyes burned with awakening desire as she turned to look at him. But she seemed to remember when he did not, why they were gathered in the pack's meeting house. So she shooed away his attentions with a small smile and a whispered promise that there would be time for more serious play after the meeting. Ivan reluctantly pulled back, eyes smoldering, but he kept her held close within the protective circle of his arms.

Gathering around them in the dimly fire lit room, were the adult members of his large family. Cousins, uncles, aunts, nieces, and nephews...they would all be in attendance. Ivan was thankful for each and every one of them, as he knew his wife was. Brianna was over seven months pregnant and heavy with the new life that grew within her. She had emigrated from the United States less than a year ago in order to be his mate—his *wife*—sacrificing much to be at his side in the wilderness of his homeland. But she had left unfinished business behind her in the country of her birth, business issues with her uncle's company, which she had inherited upon his death. This meeting among family and pack mates was to decide the outcome of some of those issues.

Ivan's mother, Servinaa, cleared her throat and addressed the group at large. She spoke in English for the benefit of Brianna, who had only just begun to learn their native Russian tongue. "It is obvious that Brianna cannot go. Her time is too near. What if she were to birth the baby early? We cannot afford to let a human doctor attend the birth of one of our own. She must remain here, so that we may see to her care properly, as only our kind know how." The proud Russian tones in her voice brooked no argument.

"Yes Mama, I agree with you. But what can we do? Whom can we send to take care of this business with her company? The board members of The Living Forest conservation group asked that she arrive in person for this new proposal they have come up with. It will take much persuasion to let them accept someone else in her stead. And who among us could even act with the authority that will be necessary among the professionals of New York?" Ivan argued, feeling the futility of the situation set in upon him.

"Well she cannot go. Not until after the birth of her cub, at any rate," Servinaa said.

"I could go for a few days only. They'll understand why I can't stay long after signing the necessary papers," Brianna said.

"No." From out of a darkened corner of the room came an authoritative and serious masculine voice.

There was a ripple of motion and a face appeared from the shadows. Nikolai stepped into the illumination of the fire lit room. His movements held an alien grace, full of danger, mystery and above all, power. It was no wonder why he was the most respected and feared of their kind—the Wawkalak, the Bodark, the werewolf.

Everyone in the room was moved to silence. It wasn't often that they saw Nikolai indoors like this. He was usually out in the wilderness, seeing to the protection and safety of the village and the people who dwelled within it. He was a lone wolf, a protector of their family and way of life. He was the alpha Bodark…the pack leader.

"No. Brianna, you will stay within the safety of our borders. We cannot risk you or the child that you carry." Nikolai's voice was firm and unyielding.

"Then what shall we do, Nikolai? Her people need her signed approval to continue their efforts to save the ancient American forests. We must not stand in the way of such a noble endeavor. It is our duty to care for the Earth mother, whether in our own borders or across the sea."

"You are right, Ivan. These legal papers must be signed. The ancient forests of the world must be saved," Nikolai agreed somberly.

"But the board won't send me the papers to sign. They want someone there in person to hear the proposal and to clear up the rest of my uncle's unfinished business within the company. I've put it off for so long that they're not taking any excuses this time. I have to go," Brianna pointed out.

"You will not go, and that is final." Nikolai waited a long beat before he spoke again. It seemed that he waged some internal battle before phrasing the words, "I will go." There was an audible intake of breath at his declaration.

"No! You must not leave us," interjected one of the men, a second cousin to Ivan. "You are our alpha Bodark, our leader. You cannot leave us unprotected."

"Calm yourself, Dimitri." Nikolai gave the man a hard look and Dimitri immediately shrank back into himself. He slowly, cautiously, retreated back into the shadows, obeying the compulsion in Nikolai's tone and showing his subservience to his leader. "The pack will not be unprotected. Ivan and Hugh are the pack's beta males, my seconds. They will see to things while I am away."

"I'll give you power of attorney for this project, and I will try to convince the board to let you sign in my stead. If it will make them feel safer, I can promise to attend the board meetings through speakerphone while you're in New York. I'll have to make the arrangements, but surely they would understand the necessity in this instance," Brianna said, eager to find some resolution to the problem.

"Call your people. Let them know I am coming." Nikolai's tone was final.

His word was law.

* * * * *

"Something troubles you, Niki."

Nikolai turned with a soft exhalation of breath and smiled at his grandmother, Elizabet. She had addressed him in their native language of Russian and he responded in kind. "You know me too well, Grandmamma. But I am not overburdened so rest your worried mind on that."

Elizabet sank next to him on the giant rock that overlooked their village. Though she was eighty-four years old, she still possessed the athletic prowess of her race, and was pleased to note that her bones only creaked a little bit as she sat. She wrapped him in her arms and sighed.

Ever since the age of twelve, when he had saved his two younger brothers from death at the hands of hunters and been thrust into manhood, Nikolai had been a silent strength that guarded over her and the people of their village. It wasn't often that he seemed in need of her guidance. It both worried and pleased her that he seemed to need her now, whether he wanted to admit his need or not.

"Tell me what has you up here brooding," she urged with a small smile.

"It is difficult to explain…even to myself. I am not exactly certain that there is even a need for my—brooding—as you named it," he said with a small chuckle, drawing her closer to him. "I will be leaving these shores for the first time in my life. I have not left the pack since I became alpha and I am uneasy," he admitted quietly. "There is an unsettled restlessness in my heart and I do not know the cause. Perhaps it is the moon and nothing more." They both looked up into the starlit sky and the new moon which, even though unseen, still pulled at them.

"Do you perhaps fear that Ivan and Hugh will not be able to protect the village?"

"No. They are both my seconds in command, by right of strength and cunning. They will not fail our people, or me. That is not what concerns me, be at ease on that score." His words were spoken firmly, as if the very suggestion that Ivan or Hugh would fail at their duties was unacceptable.

They were both silent for a long moment, watching the flickering lights in the log homes down below their lofty perch.

"Why do you go, Niki? Why do you feel the need to go to this strange American city and be amongst so many humans? It is not merely to protect Brianna and her babe. That much I can see."

Nikolai seemed to weigh his words carefully before answering. "I feel that I am being led by a power that is beyond me. I have had dreams. Visions. I have had them for some time now, but only recently have they plagued me with increasing frequency. I am growing more and more restless as each night passes, and the dreams are to blame, I am sure of it. These dreams tell me now to go to America and find what destiny has in store for me there. I have to go. I will not be able to rest until I do."

"If you have had visions then you have no choice but to go where they lead you. As alpha, you have a greater gift of the far-seeing eye than any other in our pack. But what do you think you will find in America? What could possibly await you there but heartache in the midst of so many strangers? So many *humans*? Have your dreams told you that much?"

"I do not know what I will find. But I must leave this place and I must leave it soon. I feel that something is waiting for me, across the sea. It has been waiting for a long time and I must go to find it." His voice was nearly a whisper, but still firm in resolve.

Elizabet had never seen her grandson so determined. He was always sure of himself, and perhaps more than a little arrogant as alpha male of their pack. But this was something else entirely. She smiled and kissed his hair lightly. "You will do what you must, as you always have. But be careful, my grandson. You yourself have admitted that you know not what is waiting for you across the sea. Beware of danger on all sides, Nikolai. The world is not often kind, especially to beings like us. Be wary of the moon's phases—act like a human—but do not forget who and what you are. Come back to us soon."

"I will Grandmama," he promised. His pale blue eyes glittered dangerously in the moonlight. "Very soon. I promise you."

Chapter One

Waxing Moon

One month later

ꙮ

Julia Thurman rubbed at her aching temples with a weary and heartfelt sigh. She'd been working for over twelve hours without a break, seeing to the registration of several new hotel guests, as was her job. But today she was alone at the front desk, her two co-workers having called in sick with the flu...or the twenty-four hour plague, as she liked to refer to it. Friday was a busy day for her at work on a normal day, but when so many of her co-workers called in sick, as was often the case, it was a stressful endeavor at best. She hadn't even found time to eat lunch, as her rumbling tummy reminded her vociferously.

What she wanted, more than anything, was to take a vacation. A vacation to some far off place, where no one could bother her. A place where she could sit down with her favorite romance novel and read undisturbed until her heart was content. But, alas, she couldn't afford it—not on her meager salary—and especially not after her semester dues came in from the New York School of Visual Arts. It wasn't cheap, training to be a professional sculptor and painter.

Julia sighed and imagined herself back at home with her parents on their Pennsylvania ranch. When she'd lived there she had taken the quiet solitude of country living for granted, but now, after five years of living in the big city, she found she sorely missed it. The rolling hills of the pasture land, the sweet pungent odor of the manure covered cornfields, the husky aroma of the horses' stables—they were all a treasured memory now. How she wished she could return.

But her parents were dead, both from strokes only one year apart, and the ranch had been auctioned to clear their debts. What little money had remained, she'd used to move to the big city—a lifelong dream—and now, at the age of 25, after much hard work and penny pinching, she was enrolled in one of the best art schools in the United States. It was costly, but it was enriching and the dream of one day being a professional artist was all that kept her going on days such as this one.

Julia sighed again and bent back to her work, brushing away the brooding thoughts that could only serve to make her more frustrated. Her dark, dishwater blonde hair chose that moment to fall over her face and she gritted her teeth in frustration. Her hair was so thick its weight often escaped from the clips she used to secure it back from her face. She'd thought more than once of getting her waist-length tresses cut short, but knew her natural curl would only spring around her head in an Afro if she did. With practiced ease she refastened her unruly hair into its alligator clip, all the while wishing futilely for a straight, sleek mane. That thought led to another, then another, and before long Julia remembered the one thing she'd been avoiding thinking about all week.

Tomorrow night at nine she would be drink hostess at The Living Forest reception party. It was to be a formal affair and she wouldn't be able to get away with wearing her usual work livery of black slacks and a black sports jacket. She would have to dig up a formal dress somewhere.

Julia didn't *do* formal affairs. Not very well, at any rate.

But the extra money for the three hours spent in the hotel's ballroom would see her through the next month's rent on her tiny efficiency apartment. And the tips! She'd worked a similar soiree a few months past with the conservation group and the tips alone were a wonderful bonus. She might be able to afford that large set of *Windsor and Newton* oils she'd been eying at the art supply store, as well as some much needed stretched canvas and *Plaster of Paris*. The money she earned should make all the trouble of prepping herself for the event worthwhile.

She'd have to have her hair done in a way that would hold well for a few hours—if that were even possible. The cost for that would be thirty bucks plus a tip at her local beauty parlor, if she was lucky. And she would have to stop by a department store to have her make-up applied at one of the cosmetic make over counters. The cost for that should be nil, as long as she didn't give in to the sales-persons urgings to buy the products they used on her face. That wouldn't be too hard. Julia rarely if ever wore make up. She couldn't even put the stuff on properly, a shameful thing for her artist's pride to admit, even if only to herself. The thought made her grimace with a bit of shame in her lack of femininity.

It wasn't easy being a plain Jane. But not everyone could be drop-dead gorgeous like half the ladies in New York City seemed to be. Julia just wished that for once she could *feel* like an attractive woman, instead of an awkward bookworm with paint and plaster under her nails more often than not. For once she wanted to be the woman pursued by all the eager men. To see what it was like to be wanted by a lusty male. But, she reminded herself, it would be harder to reassume her role as the lonely dowd if she were to have that one, decadent, taste. Harder to shrink back into the shadows of her anonymity after knowing the carnal pleasures to be had in a man's arms.

It was best not to dwell on that daydream. No matter how pleasant the images in her mind might be.

Better to live vicariously through her romance novels. The reality of a great romance was just not for her. That was something she was most definitely sure of. Dominant, virile men did not go for the plain-faced, large breasted, thick-hipped woman. In stories they might, but not in real life. And while she'd had her opportunities for affairs with a string of nerd jerks, small-minded simpletons, or weak-willed mama's boys, Julia just couldn't bring herself to accept their offers. She was a little more discerning in her choice of bed partners at this point in her life. She just wasn't ready to settle her expectations so low quite yet.

Perhaps after another few lonely years, she would be more amiable to the idea. But not now. While her expectations weren't too high—she would be more than content to hook up with a shy, brainy type like herself after all—it seemed that for now what she wanted could not be found in the great city in which she lived. Men like that had been taken long ago, and all the good-looking, stud-muffin ones were either gay or off chasing the seemingly endless supply of sleek model types. She would have to be content to stay on her own…or submit to the greasy, pawing types that were always, not surprisingly, available.

The phone rang at her elbow, startling her out of her musings.

"Thank you for calling Drayton Towers Hotel. This is Julia. How may I help you?"

"Julia, I'm so glad you answered instead of the boss. Listen, I'm coming down with something so I won't be able to make it in tonight. Can you cover for me?"

Julia gritted her teeth. "George, you called in last Friday. Don't you think it's a little unfair to do this again?"

"I wasn't sick last Friday. I had a dentist appointment," George said in a cajoling whine.

"And I have yet to see that dentist's written excuse you promised me."

"Aw, quit acting like a shift manager and be a pal. I really do feel bad." George gave some very obviously fake coughs to back up his claim.

"Why don't I believe you, George?" Julia asked in exasperation. "Wait a minute—is that music I hear playing in the background?" She listened harder and heard the low murmur of several people. "And are those voices I hear, too? I thought you lived alone?"

"I can't get by you, can I Julia? You're too smart for me. Look, you're right, I'm not sick. But I really do need you to cover for me tonight. I'm at this party and there's this girl, oh man is she hot—"

"Listen, George, I've been here since seven this morning. Seven! I was supposed to get off work at three this afternoon. Betty called in and Tom called in—I've been working by myself all day. I'm tired, I'm hungry and I have a portrait due in class on Monday. I need my free time, George, just like you do. Now get your butt in here and work or so help me—"

"Go ahead and write me up again if it will make you feel better. But I can't come in tonight, I really can't. If you'll let me slide this one time, I promise you Julia—I *promise*—that I'll cover for you whenever you need me to. Any day you want. Just let me skip out tonight, 'kay? Pretty please?"

"I will write you up and I will definitely tell Mr. Morlock if you don't show tonight, George. I mean it. I'm not a machine, I can't work all these long hours."

"I'm only scheduled from seven to eleven tonight. What's four more hours when you've worked all day anyway? And don't tell me you have plans—you never have plans."

"You try working a twelve hour shift on the busiest day of the week and then tell me how you feel about working four more hours on top of it! I'm exhausted, George, and I want to go home at a decent hour tonight."

"But you need the money don't you? Just grab a book and hide behind the desk until the shift is over. It won't be too bad."

"It's not that easy, George, or you would be in here working like you're supposed to. Now, please get in here and work your shift."

George affected a long-suffering sigh. Julia gritted her teeth, surprised that they didn't crumble, so hard did she clench her jaw. He wasn't going to show. She knew it. He didn't care about his paycheck enough to worry about getting written up—again. One more written warning after this and he would be fired. Not that it mattered. His parents took care of all his finances. This job was just gravy money to him. If the world were fair he would care that his laziness was going to cost her some much needed study-time.

But the world wasn't fair.

"I'm sorry you're not willing to help me out here, Julia. I thought we were buddies, but I guess I was wrong. Go ahead and write me up because I'm not coming in tonight. I've got better things than to hang around that place on a Friday night. See ya." The phone clicked in her ear as George hung up.

Julia rubbed her temples. "Calm blue ocean, calm blue ocean—think of a calm blue ocean, Jules." She continued to repeat her mantra, taking deep, soothing breaths.

Calming her anger was not an easy thing to do, but she managed after several moments. Then, dislodged with the motions of her fingers at her temples, her hair fell heavily into her face once more. "Oooooh!" she screeched, yanking the oversized alligator clip out of her hair.

Unfortunately, she thought with a whimper, *the night has only just begun.*

* * * * *

8:30 p.m.

Julia sighed, sending a puff of air up into a stray lock of hair that had fallen over her face, making it dance. Time was just not passing quickly enough for her. Luckily though, the amount of new arrivals for check in had slowed considerably along with the passage of time and she was afforded the rare opportunity to actually *sit* in her chair behind the reception desk. Her boss, Mr. Morlock, had already left for the evening, sympathetic enough with her plight to help her write up the missing George, but not sympathetic enough to hang around and help her out on her shift. He, like everyone else she knew, had plans for the night that couldn't—or wouldn't—be broken.

Julia's stomach gave a loud rumble, reminding her that she hadn't eaten all day. She'd neglected to bring along a sandwich for lunch, expecting—foolishly—that she'd get off of work on time so that she could eat her meal in the quiet comfort of her apartment. With no small amount of chagrin, she realized that she should have planned on staying late from the beginning. She knew her co-workers all too well to harbor the hope that no one would call in sick on a Friday. Well, she was paying for her own naïveté now and she hoped her grouchy tummy could wait just a couple more hours until it was fed. Unfortunately, she didn't have the money to blow on ordering take-out just now.

Hunching her shoulders to easy the empty ache in her middle, she bent back to flip through the fashion magazine she'd found buried in a cubby hole beneath the counter, pausing now and again to draw a bushy moustache or armpit hair on the forms and features of the models. Julia couldn't help but grimace, as page after page was revealed, laden with advertisements featuring half naked, willow thin models. God, if only she could be so lucky. She sighed, then gave a small giggle at her overly morose thoughts, adding some potbellies and double chins to the lovely men and women for good measure.

It was then that the back of her neck prickled with a sudden, disturbing unease. Someone was watching her. Staring at her. She could actually feel the person's gaze, like a heavy, laden weight on her bent head. Slowly, with a heart that was already inexplicably pounding, she raised her head to see whom the disturbing gaze belonged to.

Less than twenty feet away stood a man. A very big man.

Oh lord, she thought, as the bottom of her stomach landed with a plop somewhere in the vicinity of her feet. *He's amazing!*

Dressed from head to toe in deep black clothing, standing tall and straight, he seemed to swallow all of the surrounding light in the hotel lobby. He stood so still that for an odd moment he appeared to her a lifeless stone statue. The man seemed truly otherworldly, in his stillness and in his stance. Then she saw the rise and fall of his chest as he breathed and the moment passed. Julia couldn't help but let her eyes rove over him, eating him up in the only way she knew she'd ever be allowed to. His head was slightly bent, leaving most of his face in shadow and his long golden hair framed his face, trailing down over the rich velvet lapels of his stylish overcoat. But his eyes—his icy blue eyes—positively blazed out like beacons from the darkness hiding his face.

And those gorgeous eyes were locked dead-on with hers.

The empty ache in her stomach intensified, then was replaced with the frantic, psychotic flapping of butterflies' wings. To her dazed mind, it felt as if a thread were being drawn taught between her gaze and the stranger's and she could not for the life of her pull free from it. Her heart raced in an almost painful cadence and she grew feverishly lightheaded. It took every ounce of her strength and will to draw a breath to steady her racing nerves.

The sudden, ragged sound of her indrawn breath did not go unnoticed by the man, if the widening and darkening of his eyes were any indication, and Julia was sure they were. Her cheeks burned with a sudden blush of embarrassment.

Julia was startled and amazed when he suddenly appeared directly in front of the desk. Even though her eyes had never left him, she had failed somehow to see his approach. One second he was across the lobby over ten feet away, and the next he was leaning down over her desk, hands splayed wide to brace himself on the counter top. It was like stop-motion film. He simply just *appeared*, almost on top of her. Strangely enough this both terrified and excited her.

Her first instinct, one ultimately of survival, was to push away from the desk and run for her life, especially after his abrupt and unexpected movement. But the thread that held her gaze to his was still there and would not break, so it was impossible for her to flee. In the back of her befuddled mind she heard her renewed, breathless pants, and knew she must look like a besotted fool. But she couldn't control her helpless reaction to him no matter how much she wanted to.

The man was drop-dead, lip licking, gorgeous. Almost too handsome for her to look at him comfortably, his masculine beauty was just that breathtaking. His sharp, rugged features were both dangerous and sexy. His skin was tanned, but not with the smooth unblemished look one had from lying beneath tanning lights in a salon or spa. No, this was obviously the careless and incredibly sexy tan of a man who spent too much of his time out under the natural rays of the sun. His long golden hair was streaked from it as well, beginning in a lovely widows peak upon his high, broad brow and ending just a bit past his shoulders.

His eyebrows were artful black slashes above his wintry eyes, their dark color contrasting quite noticeably beneath the tawny gold of his hair. His soot colored lashes seemed ten miles long and were tipped with a similar gold. His nose was strong and straight, his mouth was lush and decadently sculpted—made perfect for kissing she had no doubt. The column of his throat drew her attention especially, that strong ridge of tendon and sinew that led into the broadest shoulders she'd ever seen in her life. Underneath his stylish Armani suit and overcoat she could clearly see that he was heavily muscled, with the powerful body of an athlete, and he held himself with such grace that Julia instinctively knew he hadn't earned his physique in a gym. He was far too comfortable in his skin to have been vain enough to work for his heavy form. He'd been born lucky enough to grow into it naturally.

Julia would have done anything for the chance to paint him. To capture such a wild and untamed masculinity such as the one he possessed would have been a priceless challenge.

The man oozed a potent animal magnetism and it was plain to see that he would be one of great carnal appetites. And he was eyeing her like he wanted to gobble her up at his next meal. Julia hoped and prayed she didn't stutter when it came time to gather her wits and actually *speak* to him. Opening her mouth like a fish out of water, she searched for the proper and professional words that had been ingrained in her these past few years at the hotel in order to greet him. She was stunned anew when the man bent even closer and…*sniffed* her.

As strange as the moment was, as much as she wanted to flee for safety or better yet throw herself into his arms and what had to be certain danger, Julia couldn't move away more than a few scant inches. The man's nostrils flared as he breathed deep. His pale, pale eyes shuttered as he scented her hair, her neck and the air over her visibly shuddering chest.

The stranger was bent completely over the counter, his body otherwise utterly still. How much time passed, Julia couldn't have said, but the strange man seemed oblivious to their surroundings. With a soft, low growl—a sound startlingly alien and feral—the man leaned even closer so that only the space of a breath separated them. She could feel the moist warmth of his breath and smell his wild, tangy scent. Desire and trepidation swamped her until she feared she would pass out. She was like a deer caught in the hunter's spotlights, unable to run, unable to even think. Anticipation of his next move consumed her and her vision swam drunkenly.

Without meaning to, without even knowing she was capable of it, she leaned closer to him, meeting him halfway. Their lips were separated now by nothing more than a hairsbreadth. She tasted the sweet spice of his breath and knew that he could taste hers in turn. She wanted to shut her eyes, to give in to the temptation of closing that last miniscule distance between them, and press their mouths together. But her eyes were caught and held open by his and he seemed to reach into the depths of her with that gaze, laying her bare and open before him, so that she was forced to let him keep command of the situation.

It was the most wondrously seductive moment of her life.

The stranger muttered something in a foreign, exotic tongue, breathing the word into her mouth. His voice was deep and entrancing, and the sound of it echoed through her head long after his lips had ceased moving. Her eyes burned and the aching in her heart grew in intensity. Whatever he had said, and she hadn't the faintest idea what it was, it had drawn that invisible link between them even tighter. In that moment she wanted to be his with a fierceness she'd never known in all her life. She wanted to belong to him in the most earthy and elemental of ways. It would break her heart if she couldn't find a way to be wholly and utterly *his*. It was foolish to feel such a link with this stranger, but Julia was helpless to fight against its strength.

His heavily lashed eyes were still slightly shuttered, veiling his almost glowing gaze with a lush curtain of blond-tipped kohl, as he slowly closed the last minute distance between them. In the back of her mind she noted the rakish silver loop that pierced his ear, and the claw shaped tigers eye stone that dangled from it. Until the last, she thought he meant to kiss her, and she wanted him to kiss her with every last fiber of her being. But he moved slightly to the side and Julia was given no warning other than the sight of the stranger's lips parting. He swooped in and licked her cheek with one long, velvet swipe of his tongue.

Oh God, but that was even better than a kiss! As strange as it was—his licking her, *marking her*—the caress seemed far more intimate and erotic than any kiss she could have imagined. Julia was nearly undone as she felt his tongue lave her flesh and an arousal so fierce she would have screamed with it had she been able, swept through her like wildfire. In that moment—for the first time ever in her life—she was swept away by passion's fierce current, and had the stranger commanded it she would have spread herself wide for his pleasure with no thought to the consequences. In that instant she was but a slave to his potent and magnetic allure, unprepared in her innocence to deal with such a raw and instant attraction.

She loved every crazy, forbidden moment of it.

The man pulled away, but only slightly, and gazed intently into her eyes once more. A moment of sanity returned and she rallied the last remnants of her professionalism. It was the only armor she could erect just then between her fierce lust for him and this man's obvious interest in her. "C-can..." her voice faltered then she tried again. "Can I h-help you, sir?" She knew the question was silly and anticlimactic under the circumstance, but she also knew that she was lucky to find the wits to speak at all.

The man slowly closed his eyes, as if savoring the sound of her voice, though she knew that had to be fanciful thinking on her part. Then, just as slowly, he opened them and the blaze of his eyes was even brighter than before.

"You have already helped me more than you know," he said in that sinfully decadent voice of his. His words were lyrical in their cadence, letting her know that English was not his first language by any stretch of the imagination.

"I don't understand." She cleared her throat and straightened in her seat. In her mind she couldn't help wincing over the sudden ripe throbbing in her breasts and between her legs. "Do you have a r-reservation? Do you need a r-room?" She tried not to blush over her obvious stuttering.

The stranger's movements were slow when he pulled back, as if he were dazed or tired...or worse, in a stupor. Julia wanted to groan her disappointment when she thought that last part. It would be just her luck that the only attractive man to ever pay her any real attention in the past, well, *forever*, was drunk off his gourd.

But she didn't smell any booze on him. He smelled sweet, sinful, but not inebriated. That, at least, gave her some hope and peace of mind.

The man's gorgeous eyes were heavily lidded and he opened and closed them lazily, like a big exotic cat might be seen to do at a zoo. His sexy, gorgeous—*positively deadly*—lips smiled, slightly revealing the bright white glint of his teeth behind them.

"I have no need of a room. I already have lodgings here. I was just coming to check…" he paused and appeared to chose his next words with extra care before continuing, "and see if I could perhaps stay longer than my original plans dictated."

For a moment Julia was sure that hadn't been what the stranger had intended to say in his heavily accented tones, but he did not recant his request so she smiled and reached for the computer nearest to her. "If you'll tell me your name and room number I can change it pretty easily. If you have your cardkey on you I'll re-key it for however long you like. Oh! I almost forgot. I'll need your credit card, too, so I can reserve the funds on your account." She silently thanked the heavens that she was no longer stuttering.

"My room number is 1203." He handed her the cardkey to his room, along with his credit card. "My name is Nikolai Tamits." He paused for a moment. "What is your name?"

Julia felt the lunatic grin that spread over her face when he asked her the question. She tried not to blush on top of everything, but knew that she had failed when her cheeks heated under the intense regard of Nikolai's pale aquamarine eyes. "Julia Thurman," she said, more than a little breathless and helplessly chagrined because of it.

"Julia…" He seemed to savor the feel and sound of her name on his tongue. "Julia. In the Latin language your name means one who is youthful and soft-haired." His eyes strayed across the curves of her face and the heavy tresses on her head.

"I think your name suits you more than even your parents might have intended when they called you thus."

What a slick-tongued devil this foreign man was, Julia thought with an inner smile. "Do you memorize the meanings of women's names so you can recall their meanings at just the right moment?" She arched an eyebrow and knew her smile was a teasing one but couldn't have helped it had she tried.

"I read it once in a book and for some reason I could never understand I remembered it. Perhaps anticipation of this meeting was the very reason I did." His eyes burned as they practically ate the clothes off of her.

Julia shifted, a bit nervous under the intensity of his gaze. She kept swinging from extreme arousal to nervousness then to an instinctive, borderline fear as he continued to stand there and look her over from her head down to her midriff. The rest of her body disappeared behind the desk, and she had no doubt he'd be looking even further if he could.

"Well you're certainly smooth, I'll give you that." She had to forcibly tear her eyes away from his lips and throat, which seemed to constantly demand her attention, and focus on her work at the computer. In the back of her mind she rejoiced in her sudden newfound ability to talk lightly with Nikolai—she'd never come so close to flirting in her life and it was a liberating experience. "How much longer do you intend to stay? I can program your card key for up to another week but after that you'll have to come back and have it re-programmed again."

"I am not certain how long my…business will take before it is completed. Can I just have you give me the week and if I wish to check out before then come by and turn it in?"

"Absolutely. And rest assured that your credit card won't be charged until you check out, so if you leave early it won't be a problem to calculate your bill accordingly. I assume you wish to stay in the same room? You can change if you like of course—"

"I would like to keep the same room, if you do not mind. It has a lovely balcony and I enjoy watching the night sky unfold over the tall buildings of your city. It is quite soothing."

Julia loved the exotic cadence of his voice, could have listened to it for ages, but all too quickly her fingers flew over the keyboard and in less than a minute his stay at their hotel had been successfully extended a week. Almost reluctantly she handed back his credit card and room key. His long, strong fingers caressed over hers as he reached to take the items, and a shudder of pure longing wracked her body.

"Have dinner with me tonight, fair Julia of the soft hair."

If the world had stopped spinning on its axis she wouldn't have been more surprised than she was upon hearing his words. If he hadn't mentioned her name in the charmingly eloquent request she would have looked around to make sure he was actually speaking to her. "With m-me?"

"With you. Only you." A devilish twinkle entered his eyes then, lending him a less dangerous and more boyish quality.

Dinner with the sexiest man she'd ever clapped eyes on? Was there a chance in hell she would—*could*—say no? Then, her heart fell as she remembered how late it would be before she could leave work...and how empty her pocket book was to boot. The only restaurants that would be open so late would be very expensive indeed.

"I don't get off work until eleven. And I doubt I'd look good in my work uniform in any respectable restaurant just now." She laughed nervously, a little shamefaced that she would never be worldly or comfortably rich enough to play in the big leagues as this man probably did.

"I do not care if you have to work until three in the morning, so long as you will share a meal with me. As for your clothes, you look delectable as you are, but if it makes you feel more comfortable we can eat on my balcony and I will order us some room service. Whatever you like, it will be...*my treat,* as you Americans say."

Oh, how tempting it was to accept his offer. She barely knew him, true, but wouldn't it be lovely to get to know him better? And better, and better if she were lucky. She almost laughed in giddy excitement at the thought of having this incredibly sexy man all to herself tonight. Any moment she feared she'd wake up and find this whole exchange a dream, a hopeless fantasy, thanks to a deprived and overtired mind.

Before she even planned to say the words she heard herself say, "Okay. That sounds great. I'll just come up to your room when I get off work then, shall I?"

"I will come down and escort you," he promised in a velvet voice.

Julia shivered again and watched, dazed, as he captured her hand and lifted it to his lips. He first smelled her skin, inhaling deeply through his nostrils, then darted his tongue out to taste her. She almost fainted with shock and desire. Then he pressed his lips fervently to her hand. His lips were like silk and scorching hot against her and she felt the slight rasp of his evening whiskers. It seemed forever that he held her there against his mouth, then, as if he wasn't happy with only the kiss, she felt the small, faint prick of his teeth as he softly bit into the softness of her flesh.

Nikolai pulled back but kept her hand held captive in his. He turned her hand over and let his strong, faintly callused thumb scrape slowly, lingeringly, over the frantic beat of her pulse in her wrist. Then he bent and pressed a quick, hard kiss to the palm of her hand, closing her fingers over it when he pulled away. "Until later, Julia. Do not forget our date. I will be here promptly at eleven." Then, as if the hounds of hell were on his heels, he rushed to the elevator at the other end of the lobby, stepped into it and was gone.

As if she could forget. Odds were she'd remember that kiss on her hand for the rest of her life.

Julia squealed, hopped up from her chair and did a little dance around it before settling back down with a lunatic grin playing on her face. Thank goodness George had taken the night off!

Chapter Two

ꟹ

The rest of Julia's shift passed by with unbearable slowness for her. The steady ebb and flow of new arrivals dwindled to a trickle, making the time seem to stretch on even longer. Julia did everything she could to pass the time. She read, she cleaned, she sketched, and she counted the squares on the geometrically designed carpet beneath her feet. But alas her self-appointed busy work only served to fill in a short amount of time, or so it seemed to her eager mind and heart. She was just too excited about her anticipated evening to keep from looking at her watch every few moments, an action that was sure, in and of itself, to make the time seem to crawl by ever more slowly.

After what seemed like an endless eternity, Julia's watch read that it was no less than twenty minutes until her shift ended and one of her co-workers arrived to relieve her of her post.

"Hi Julia. Looks like George bailed on you again, huh?"

Julia smiled at Nora as she joined her behind the reception desk. Nora was a lovely, youthful thirty-something aspiring actress "slash" model. And she was just as lovely on the inside as she was outside. Julia liked her very much and knew that although she wasn't often successful in finding work in her chosen field, she was nevertheless worthy of her aspirations.

"Yeah, you guessed it right the first time."

"Why didn't you call me? I would have come in earlier."

Julia hadn't called Nora because she knew that she'd been spending the evening with her young daughter. Nora worked two full time jobs when she wasn't lucky enough to have a modeling gig—the better to support herself and her spunky six year old—and Julia wouldn't have taken away what precious time Nora had at home no matter how tired she was. "Well I figured I could use the extra cash, you know? And I knew you and Amy were going to have dinner tonight before you came in."

"Oh Julia, you're such a sweetheart to remember that. But I would have come in if you'd needed me."

"I know you would have and that's why I didn't call." The two women smiled at one another. "How is Amy doing?" Julia asked.

"Great. She's had one of her finger paintings hung in the hallway for parent teacher night next week."

"That's great. I'll bet she's really excited."

"Oh yeah. She's been talking about it non-stop for the past two days." Nora laughed, a husky, breathless sound that on anyone else might have sounded over-practiced, but it was all part and parcel of who Nora was.

"I remember the first time I had one of my drawings hung up in school. I was so proud. I was in kindergarten too, but I'll never forget how thrilling it was to have perfect strangers come through and see my work."

"One day you'll have that, only it'll be hundreds—thousands—that see your work. Can you imagine how excited you'll be then?"

Julia smiled back, marveling at how sincere and positive Nora could be when she talked about her art. But she'd always been that way, and when Julia had given Nora a painting of her and little Amy the previous Christmas, Nora had grown even more encouraging and generous with her praise. "And one day you'll be a star yourself, gracing the pages of every slick fashion magazine."

Nora sighed and with a tired little smile she sat in a chair next to Julia. "It's fun to dream, isn't it? But I do have some news—I'll be in the Fall *Aurora* catalog. It's not much but it'll keep the bill collectors at bay for a few months."

"That's great! *Aurora* is a big department store and a lot of posh people shop there. The exposure for the magazine could be great for you."

"I know, but I'm trying to play it down so I don't get my hopes up, ya know?"

Unfortunately Julia *did* know, all too well. In the big city of New York, it was never good to count ones chickens before they hatched. And that was especially true of anyone in the arts or entertainment industry. There were just too many people around in that field to assume that any one person could shine like a diamond amongst them without having made it somewhere else first. It was hard to break into mainstream, harder than anyone outside of the business could imagine.

Julia smiled in sympathy and understanding then remembered her own good news. "Oh Nora, you won't believe what just happened to me tonight." She proceeded to divulge to her friend the details of her meeting with the dangerous and exotic Nikolai Tamits in room 1203 and his romantic and unexpected dinner proposal.

"Oh, I've seen him Jules and he's a total hottie! Betty and I worked the shift he checked in on last week. He usually comes in late at night, alone, and heads up to his room without even stopping to ask if he's received any messages. Betty and I thought he was gay at first because he barely spared us more than a passing glance when we checked him in."

"Now you're just saying that to build up my ego, so I'll feel honored that he asked me to dinner when he could have asked you or the lovely—*gag!*—Betty." Julia rolled her eyes exasperatedly.

"No, I'm telling you the truth. Betty was making goo-goo eyes at him the entire time but he barely looked at her. He looked at me—politely is all I can say about it—but that look made my knees turn to water right on the spot even if he wasn't meaning for it to, and I'm sure he wasn't. I'm so glad to hear that you caught his eye, it's so exciting! When was the last time you went out on a date? A real date, I mean, not an outing with a classmate or whatever."

Julia thought for a moment and was more than a little chagrined to realize that she couldn't precisely remember when she'd last gone out with anyone. "High school I think." She laughed at Nora's shocked expression. "But it's mostly because I just haven't had the time to pursue the opposite sex with all the work I've been doing since I moved here, preparing for school and whatnot."

"Honey, no matter how hard I work I always have time to pursue the opposite sex," Nora said in a deliberately sexy drawl. "If I didn't then I wouldn't have my baby girl now would I? And Lord knows that she's my pride and joy. Were would I be without her? I'd be as lonely as you are—no offense."

"None taken. I am lonely sometimes, but I handle my life the only way I know how and unfortunately or fortunately, however you want to look at it, that leaves little time for me to date or play hanky panky. Plus the only men who ever show an interest in having a relationship or, at the least, bumping uglies with me are usually the kind I try my best to steer clear of."

"Oh honey, you're just never around the right men, that's your problem. If you'd make time to go out on the town you'd find some downright hunky men who'd give anything to 'bump uglies'," Nora snickered at the phrase, "with you."

"I don't care about the hunky part so much as I care about the 'give anything' part. I don't want a slave, don't get me wrong, but I do want a man who's not unwilling to work his way up to earning my heart. I want a man, a good man, who'll love me no matter how I look in the early morning hours, who'll rub my feet after I've been on them all day and so on and so forth. I want a man who'll want me, not just for sex, but also for conversation—*intelligent* conversation. Someone who'll try to bring down the moon should I want it and cherish me forever through thick and thin. That's what I want."

The two friends sighed dreamily.

"But honey," Nora said gently, "men like that are few and far between—if they even exist at all beyond the covers of a romance novel. Why not set your sites a little lower? You might not find the great, magical romance of your dreams, but at least you'll find happiness. Don't shut out your chance at contentment with a normal, flawed, man and wait in vain for the gentle perfect knight on a white charger. They just don't exist."

"I know that. But I'm not ready to stop dreaming that there might be, somewhere out there, the perfect man for me. When I'm ready to settle down I'll set aside my silly dreams but for now..."

"Yeah, I understand. Like I said, it *is* fun to dream. Now, let's change the subject, I'm getting too depressed. Have you got any clothes to change into for this date?"

"No. I'm going to have to wear this. At least it's black. I'll need all the slimming down I can get, whether it's a visual trick or not."

"Oh shut up about your weight, Jules. You're not fat. You're curvy. There's a big difference."

"Wow, thanks for the pep-talk Nora. Coming from someone as skinny and statuesque as you that makes me feel oh so much better."

"Quit looking like you've just eaten a lemon. Your face will freeze that way if you keep it up. Didn't your mother ever tell you that? Anyway, I can't help it that I'm like I am—I'm not a health fanatic that's for sure—I'm just lucky that my metabolism is so high because I eat like a horse. It's good genes I guess."

"My heart bleeds for you, it really does," Julia joked.

"Oh hush. And really, you don't need to be so hard on yourself about your appearance. I've seen how you hunch all the time to hide your chest, you need to stand up straighter and flaunt those puppies. I wish I were as well endowed as you. But," she sighed for dramatic effect, "I guess someone has to help Victoria's Secret stay in business. Thank goodness for Miracle bras."

"I don't hunch to hide, I hunch because they're so frickin' heavy." Julia said this with a straight face but couldn't help laughing when Nora choked and sputtered in her own surprised mirth.

"Ah, Jules you always make me laugh." Nora wiped a tear from her eye with an artfully manicured hand. "But seriously, you're too hard on yourself about your looks."

"I'm not really that concerned with my looks, or at least I didn't used to be. But I grew up in a small country town where image meant less than nothing so my weight and build were never an issue. But after coming here…"

"Everyone is concerned with image here. It's hard not to notice that and get caught up in it." Nora finished for her with a wise look in her eyes.

"Exactly. I'm still adjusting to that. The first week I lived here I was turned away from I don't know how many jobs and I know it was because I didn't look like I belonged here. I could see it in the way people looked at me, like I was a stray wet dog. I immediately had to change my wardrobe and start wearing my hair differently. I would have starved if I hadn't."

"Well I'm glad you got a job here. You're a lot of fun, Jules. And one day you'll meet the right guy, someone who'll make you very happy to just be yourself. Who knows…maybe that guy is Nikolai Tamits?"

"I don't know. I very highly doubt it. But it'll sure be fun finding out." Julia affected her most wicked grin.

"Ain't that the truth, honey? Hell, that's the kind of experimentation that spices up a woman's life."

Julia spent the next few moments straightening the work area and joking with Nora about inconsequential things. But all the while she was trying her best to tamp down on the rising excitement that raced through her whenever she thought about what might happen in the hours ahead. The anticipation alone was whipping her into a frenzy. She was almost dancing on her toes as she went about her final shift-change duties.

Julia was in the office situated just behind the receptionist area, squaring away the register earnings she'd accumulated during her long day, when she heard Nikolai's voice through the open door.

"I'm looking for Ms. Julia Thurman. Is she still here?"

"Yeah, she's just finishing up in the back. I'll get her for you." Julia let Nora come into the office and get her, not wanting to seem over eager to the sexy Nikolai by following her first impulse, which was to vault from the room with an excited smile on her face.

"He's here! Hurry up, girl, before he gets away," Nora whispered excitedly.

"How do I look?"

"Good enough to eat. Now go get 'em. And for God's sake, hold your shoulders straight. Make his mouth water!"

Julia muffled a laugh with her hand, straightened her shoulders as Nora had instructed, and walked out to meet her date for the evening.

Sure enough, as Nora had obviously intended—the woman knew entirely too much about men—Nikolai's eyes went straight to her breasts. And stayed there. Julia sent a quick glance to Nora, who gave her a sly wink and a smile, before she walked around the desk.

He was so much taller, so much broader than she would have thought, but when they'd met before she had been sitting behind a counter and he had been leaning low over it. Now that she stood next to him—a unique thrill all its own—she realized that he had several inches on her in height. It made her feel positively dwarfed, which wasn't necessarily a bad thing in Julia's opinion. Perhaps, given his large size, he wouldn't find her all that large in comparison. Maybe he'd find her merely...curvy. He was dressed differently now than he had been earlier, in a loose fitting, gray button up shirt and black slacks. The strong line of his jaw was freshly shaven and she could smell the very faint scent of his spicy aftershave. Though she'd found his whiskered look irresistibly sexy, she was impressed that he'd bothered to groom himself so thoroughly for her.

"Are you ready to dine, fair Julia? I find I am positively famished."

Julia didn't fail to notice that his eyes barely strayed up from her breasts as he spoke to her. For the first time in her adult life she felt truly powerful in her voluptuous femininity. She decided to savor every last moment of it. "I'm ready. Shall we go?"

Nikolai took her hand and laid it in the crook of his arm. With anyone else the gesture might have seemed a little overdone, but it seemed a normal and almost reflexive move on his part. He finally dragged his eyes away from her chest and turned to lead them towards the elevator. Julia spared one last glance back at her friend and gave her what she knew was a silly and excited grin. Nora returned the look, bounced in her seat happily, and waved them off as they strode away.

The doors closed around them, cutting them off from the outside world. Julia found herself eager to start off the night's adventure. It had been far too long since she'd felt so excited, so anticipatory of a dinner date, and she reveled in the joy of the moment. There was little doubt in her mind that the night would prove to be well worth the long day she'd just had.

Chapter Three

ꝺ

The door to Nikolai's room closed softly behind them as they stepped from the elevator and into his luxury suite. Julia felt suddenly shy now that they were completely alone in his lair. She looked around the room, not unfamiliar with her surroundings considering how long she'd worked in the hotel and how many times she'd helped in housekeeping to earn extra money. It was a large suite, larger than her apartment and, of course, considerably more comfortable. There was a living/meeting area with a deeply cushioned leather couch and recliner situated in front of a television set. There was a coat closet just behind her, next to the door where Nikolai was standing. The living room led off into a bedroom, which had a lovely little balcony, complete with a small breakfast table and a littering of flowering plants and vines that were constantly being cared for by the hotel groundskeepers. A good-sized bathroom completed the layout of the suite, with a lovely glass-enclosed shower stall and a large, round, garden tub made perfect for luxurious bubble baths.

Julia could never have afforded to stay even a night in such a room as this one and she was a little uncomfortable knowing that, when Nikolai could obviously easily afford a couple of weeks in it. But she refused to let her ever-present worries over money taint the evening ahead of her. Nikolai didn't need to know how poor she was and perhaps he wouldn't mind such a thing if he did know. It didn't matter. The night ahead of her was all that mattered, what lay beyond that she could dwell on later. So she dragged her eyes away from the rich textures that dotted the large suite and turned, instead, to meet the gaze of her dinner partner.

His eyes were positively glowing as he stared at her.

The moment stretched on for longer than Julia found comfortable and she had to look away before she ran out of breath, so skittish and aroused did she become. If just being the focal point of his gaze could do such a number on her libido, she couldn't even imagine what would happen if he closed the distance and took her in his arms. And oh how she wanted him too…but she was getting a little ahead of herself. She had to remember not to get too carried away. She had to let the night unfold on its own and not rush things. It was better to savor than to glutton.

Or something to that effect.

Nikolai's eyes roved over her from head to toe, lingering on her eyes, lips, breasts and hips. It made her skin feel heated, the way he looked at her. Made her feel breathless and—dare she even think it?—sexy. He looked at her as if she held the answers to every question he'd ever thought to ask, as if the sun rose and set in her and her alone, as if she were his salvation…as if he were hungry and she was lunch.

Julia shivered.

Nikolai cleared his throat and looked away, noticeably tearing his eyes away from her, as if it were an almost impossible feat. "Shall we order our meal and retire to the balcony?"

"Absolutely. I'm starving."

"I can hear your stomach growling from here. When was the last time you ate?"

Julia blushed, not having realized that her stomach was still gurgling loud enough to be heard. She'd thought it had quieted hours ago, but admitted she'd probably only grown used to the sound after being around it all day and night. "I had toast and juice for breakfast this morning," she said in a sheepish voice.

Nikolai's eyes flashed back to hers. "Why did you wait so long to eat when you are so obviously hungry?"

Julia couldn't help but wince at his chiding tone. "I didn't have time to go out for anything, to be honest. I was supposed to get off of work this afternoon so I didn't bring my lunch, but some people called in sick and I was stuck until tonight."

"Well you need to eat and eat well. You know the menu here, I am sure, so you must tell me if there is anything you do not want. I am famished myself so I will just order one of everything."

One of everything! Their menu was extensive and Julia did know it well, though she'd never eaten anything on it, so costly were the dishes. "I'll just have a steak if you don't mind."

Nikolai picked up the phone and dialed the number for room service. He ordered one of everything, as he'd said he would, making sure to throw two large sirloins into the order. Nikolai placed his hand over the phone and turned to her again. "How would you like yours prepared?"

"Very well done please. Almost burnt," she answered.

Nikolai repeated her preference into the phone and added his own. "I would like one of those steaks extra rare, just barely warmed. Yes, I would like it very nearly raw." He continued for a few moments then placed the phone in its cradle.

"Come outside, I have a need to see the sky," he said and Julia could almost have sworn he was a little breathless. She could have fooled herself into thinking that her mere presence affected him so noticeably, but something else—perhaps the way he held himself, so controlled and still—made her think his breathless state was due to something else. Something more serious.

She hoped he didn't have any health conditions. He looked healthy enough. Very healthy, in fact. But you never could accurately guess such things just by looking at someone. The thought of this obviously virile man having something so weakening as asthma or the like made her heart ache with sympathy for him. But despite his shortness of breath, Nikolai bounded up from the couch on which he'd perched when making his phone call, with a swift and nearly blurred movement. If the man were truly ill or weak, he sure didn't move like someone who was.

Nikolai shifted, again with a strange, lightning-quick ripple of muscle and limb that resembled a motion picture with too many frames removed, to come at her side. He took her arm and led her steadily into his bedroom. The sight of the bed, along with the commanding feel of this man's hand on her arm and his suddenly antsy behavior, made her heart race with a sudden, arousing, thrill of danger. But he sped on past the bed and threw open the door to his balcony, leading her out into the night.

The cool air of the evening washed over her, making her aware of the heated blush that stained her cheeks. She wondered how long it had been there, and if her partner had taken note of it—an embarrassing thought that only made her cheeks burn even more hot. Nikolai, she saw, seemed to instantly calm as he stepped with her out into the starlight. The moon, barely discernable over the bright illumination of the surrounding skyscrapers, was a fingernail-sliver in the sky and he raised his face to it. Julia was struck anew by how incredibly beautiful the man was and how savagely perfect was his profile, bathed in a silvery halo cast by the light of the night sky. Her heart stuttered at the sight.

"Ah," Nikolai breathed out in his sinfully dangerous voice. "I was feeling positively trapped in that room, weren't you?"

Julia's brows knit together. She'd thought the room was more than spacious and comfortable. But, she mused, he might be used to even larger accommodations. "I guess," she answered noncommittally.

Nikolai turned to her and opened his eyes. They seemed even more dazzling now, in the faintly lit black of the night. They positively beamed, like captured stars beneath the curtain of his hair. He smiled at her and she saw the glint of his teeth behind his kissable lips.

"I am sorry, I suppose you would not understand much…you are used to the walls of your city."

"And you're not?"

"I am more comfortable out of doors, away from the confines of stone or steel. That seems to be all that the structures are made of here, stone and glass and steel. It makes the buildings seem like cages to me at times."

"Where are you from?"

"The Ural Mountain range in Russia. I am from a small city there, well it is not really a city—not like you would think anyway—I suppose you might say it is a…village." He stumbled over the word, reminding her again that English was not his native tongue.

"What do you do there? For a living, I mean."

"I am a sort of…what is your word…governor? I make sure everyone follows the rules of the village, that everyone is safe in our borders. I settle disputes among pack mates, that sort of thing."

"Pack mates?" She laughed a little. "Citizens, you mean?"

"Yes. Of course, citizens." He laughed with her, though the sound was a little hollow.

"I'm sorry," she started, hoping she hadn't offended him by correcting his blunder.

"My English is often not so good. I do not mind you giving me the right words, Julia. It shows you are paying attention to what I am saying," he said with a toothy, boyish grin.

Julia laughed outright at that. How could she not hang on every word he said? The music of his voice alone commanded her undivided attention, not to mention his deliciously wicked accent. It positively shivered over her skin like a caress all its own.

"What has you here in New York City then? Are you here in a political capacity?"

"No, not that. I am here to take care of some business for a family member who is unable to make the trip just now."

"Oh, I'm sorry to hear that. Is your friend very sick?"

"No. She is pregnant." Nikolai laughed.

Julia laughed with him, marveling at how carefree she suddenly felt. For the moment she was content merely to be with him, out on the balcony, in the crisp, cool breeze. Nothing else seemed to matter. It was a liberating moment for her.

"Well it's certainly nice of you to come all this way for her. I hope she appreciates it," she said at last.

"Oh she does. In fact, she calls here every evening to be sure that I am still sane." He laughed at that. "Bri is truly a joy and she makes my cousin, her husband, as well as the rest of our family, very happy."

"She has business here? Is she from the States, then?"

"Originally, yes. But we are trying to cleanse her of her tawdry American ways."

Julia felt her own eyes flash hotly at his insulting words, but when he laughed at her reaction she realized he'd been teasing her with that last remark. "That wasn't funny, you know." But she couldn't help smiling back. In fact, she'd done more smiling with him in the past twenty minutes than she'd probably done all week long. It was strange, but she was growing very comfortable with him, despite the fact that they barely knew each other.

"And you—what do you do in your spare time, when you are not working long hours like you did today?" His jaw hardened when he mentioned the last.

"I go to school."

"Really? What do you study there?" He seemed genuinely interested in her answer.

Inwardly Julia winced, realizing that he might not be too impressed to know that she had aspirations of being a great artist. There were so many people in the world who claimed to be artistic that it made her feel almost ashamed to call herself one of them. In fact, oftentimes, she felt almost shunned when admitting to her creative leanings. But, hey, if he didn't like hearing the answer to his question, he should never have asked it in the first place.

"Art. I'm training to be a portraitist and a sculptor."

"Really?" He appeared as if he were truly intrigued with the idea.

"Yes. I've always done both, but I wanted to round out my skills with some professional training before I tackled the harsh competitiveness of the art world. And if I go to school and get my degree, I can always fall back on a teaching job if things get rough, you know?"

"That is impressive. Perhaps you will show me some examples of your work?"

Julia had heard that phrase far too many times in her life to take it seriously, but she humored him anyway. "Sure, if you'd like."

"I would very much like it. It would be an honor to see the wonders that your delicate hands have created. A great honor indeed."

Delicate hands? She almost laughed. A sculptor could never get by with delicate hands—their hands had to be tough as steel and stronger than that besides—a sculptor lived and died by the strength of muscle and bone in their hands. But she didn't tell him that. Let him think her delicate, it was almost flattering; she'd never been called delicate in her life.

While Julia searched for something to say in response there came a brisk knock on the door to Nikolai's suite.

"Good, the food has arrived. Would you mind if we ate it out here, my Julia?"

Julia's toes positively curled at the sound of him saying "my Julia" and she could only nod her assent. She couldn't have spoken had her life depended on it. Nikolai flashed her yet another of his sexy, toothsome grins and went to answer the door.

With a bounce she turned to the balcony rail and looked down on the traffic, ten stories below. Perhaps she *was* deprived, she thought dazedly. She'd certainly never reacted so strongly to a man before. Oh well, she decided to enjoy it while it lasted. It might be quite a long time before she had so exciting an evening again.

Nikolai returned with surprising swiftness and Julia barely had time to wipe the giddy grin from her face as she turned to watch him approach. He pushed a silver dining cart stacked full of covered dishes. He moved the cart before the small breakfast table and motioned for her to take a chair. Gallantly, he helped to seat her, placing a tray before her along with a linen napkin and some silverware.

"I hope this suits your pallet. Please, eat your fill." Nikolai moved to take his own seat, removing the silver dome from his plate and exposing the very pink flesh of his steak. Julia had never been a fan of rare cooked meat and had to hold back a grimace when he hungrily consumed his first bite. She took a bite of her own and was moved to slather it with an abundance of steak sauce.

Nikolai chuckled at the soupy mess she made of her meal. "You do not like steak, I gather?"

"Oh I like it, but only when it's covered with other stuff," she said, before taking another bite and chewing it heartily. She had to—it was tough as leather. Just as she preferred it.

Nikolai poured them both a glass of wine and they spent the rest of their meal in relative silence. Surprisingly enough it was a comfortable and easy silence, as if they had known each other for years and had no need of the idle banter that new acquaintances often shared. Nikolai's main courses were followed by various others, which he demanded she share with him, beautiful creations that Julia tasted if only to try out their unique flavors, but Nikolai ate practically everything he'd ordered. Julia had never seen someone eat so much in one sitting. He was obviously possessed of a nearly endless appetite. It was amazing just to watch the man eat!

"Are you not hungry? Are the dishes not to your liking?" Nikolai asked, noticing her staring at him with wide eyes.

"I'm too full to eat anymore," she said with a grin.

"But you must make up for the meals you missed today," he urged.

"No, really, I can't eat another bite. It was really good, thank you Nikolai."

"Did you try the pork? It's tender and spiced to perfection. The salmon is very fresh and tasty as well."

Julia couldn't help but laugh as he shamelessly tried to tempt her into eating more of the heaping food before them. "I promise I can't eat anymore, Nikolai. In fact, this is the most I've eaten in one sitting in my memory. I'm positively stuffed."

Nikolai's face fell and he cocked his head to one side. The movement reminded her vaguely of something, though she couldn't remember what at the moment, and made him look absolutely adorable. "I am sorry to hear that, Julia. You really should be eating more. You are in your childbearing years and require the nutrients now more than you ever will again. I do not like to know that you often eat less than you have tonight."

Julia was taken aback by his blunt words. He'd obviously misunderstood her meaning. She didn't like to know that he thought she was neglecting herself or, worse, unable to afford enough food to sustain herself. He should know just from looking at her that she wasn't starving. Far from it.

"I eat very well, don't think I don't. Jeez, just look at me. I never thought anyone would think I wasn't eating enough—too much, yes—but never too little."

Nikolai moved his hand in a decidedly elegant and foreign movement, waving away her comments with a casual disdain. "In your country I have noticed that women are concerned with keeping themselves as thin as wraiths. You, as you should very well know, are beautiful beyond words, but still far too thin for your height. It is obvious to me that you should eat more meat, more hearty foods. Not all men are as obsessed with starving ladies as those abundant in your country. Most men like a woman with curves instead of hollows."

Beautiful beyond words? *Far too thin for her height*? Julia thought she might launch herself at him with a marriage proposal right then and there. Where had this man been all of her life?

"Well thank you for the compliment, even if it was hidden in the middle of a bunch of criticisms," Julia tossed out cheekily. She laughed outright when he blushed, seeming chagrined at her words.

"I am sorry. But I worry about you already, you see? Now please, try the...*key lime,* is it? Yes. Try the lime pie, it is very good."

Julia gave in, graciously she thought, and took a bite of the dessert as he offered it to her on the end of his fork. It was delicious.

Chapter Four

ꟿ

"Do you like living in the city very much?" Nikolai asked her much later. Dinner was long since over, and they sat speaking softly, easily, together under the faint lights of the moon and stars.

"Sometimes. Though I'm not originally from here."

"Are you not? Then where are you from?"

"Pennsylvania. I grew up on a farm there, a much different place than here let me assure you. It was almost like I suffered from culture shock when I first moved here. I'd always wanted to live in a big city, but I was unprepared for just how *big* it could be. How full of strangers and strange places."

"You actually wanted to live here? Planned to do it?" Nikolai's eyes widened when she nodded her agreement. "But why?" His voice was incredulous.

"Well, I grew up in a small town. And when I was younger, I thought that by moving to the city I would become someone more important, I guess. I'm not sure what I thought, it seems so long ago." She heard her own voice trial off pensively.

"And if you had to make the choice all over again? Would you live on your farm or in the city?" He seemed very interested in her answer.

"On the farm," she answered without pause. It was a question she'd often asked herself over the years. "Don't get me wrong," she hastened to add, "I'm not exactly unhappy here. I love going to school and lord knows I've worked hard to be able to attend. But sometimes I really miss the green of the pasture, the trees and the wide-open sky. There's a kind of simplicity, a beauty, in the country that you can't find here, not even in the parks. I really miss that sometimes, you know? The quiet solitude of it."

"Yes. I have only been here a week and already I miss the silence and seclusion of my land as well. It's too busy here…too full of motion and noise and foul smells." He paused for a long moment, as though lost deep in thought. "But will you one day return to your farm—after your schooling is complete? Do you not have family there?"

"No. My parents died some years back. It's initially why I moved here. I had to sell the farm to clear off their debts," she admitted. "I have some family there still, cousins, aunts and uncles, but no one I'm really close to anymore. I haven't had time these past few years for much in the way of visiting."

"I am sorry to hear that you are so alone." His voice was low and mournful on her behalf.

"I'm not alone. How can you be alone amongst so many people in a city like this one?" Julia waved away the topic and quickly moved on to another. "So what's your home like? Tell me more about it. Do you have family there, besides your cousin and his wife?"

Nikolai tossed back his mane of hair and laughed, letting the moment of sadness between them pass as if it had never been. "Sometimes I think I have too much family there. They are always underfoot. But I love them and would protect them with my life. And my land…I wish you could see it Julia! You would love it. My village is in the middle of an old growth forest, surrounded for miles by the biggest trees you have ever seen. There are mountains all around us, reaching tall into the heavens, and snow on the ground more often than not, painting the land with sparkling white. And the air is so clean, so crisp, it almost shocks the lungs on a cold day."

"It sounds lovely. But I have to ask—what is an old growth forest?"

"The trees are hundreds, sometimes thousands of years old, many petrified to stone. Some of the oldest trees on Earth can be found there. That is why they have grown so large; they have had the time to. Some are even as big around as a small building!"

Julia marveled that such a thing could be possible—a thousand year old tree as big around as a building. It sounded outrageous, though she vaguely remembered hearing about such forests in Washington State being harvested for their lumber. "That's amazing. I can't believe you live in such a place. I bet it's absolutely gorgeous."

"It is. There is no other place on Earth that can match its beauty, of that I am absolutely positive. I think that I will appreciate it even more when I return, after having seen such a cold, gray place as this city."

They fell into a companionable silence then, each immersed in their private thoughts. Then Julia realized how late it must be, looked at her watch and almost gasped to see that it was already well past three in the morning. "Goodness! It's so late, the time has just flown by." She rose from her seat and Nikolai was instantly at her side, though she hadn't seen him move.

"Must you go?" he asked in a quiet voice.

Julia's body positively tingled at the intimate timbre of his words and at the sudden, fierce blaze of his eyes. He was so close she could see the widening of his pupils in the silvery blue fire of his eyes. "I don't want to keep you up too late. You must have business to see to in the morning." Julia knew it was a lame excuse, but now that the moment was upon her she didn't know how to acquiesce into joining him in his bed, for if the look in his eyes was any indication, that was exactly where he wanted her to be.

"What about you? Do you have to work in the morning?" he asked, intent on her answer.

"N-no. I'm not scheduled until tomorrow evening." She was suddenly breathless.

"Then stay." He seemed to growl the words and the sound washed over her with the force of a tidal wave, sweeping her under into the depths of a dark sea of passion that was impossible for her to hide from him. "Stay," he repeated in a throaty whisper.

"I *can't*," she said and hated herself for it. Here was the chance she'd been hoping for—the opportunity to feel close to someone if for but a few short hours. But, despite her profound need and desire for this man, she knew it would spell her doom were she to give in. There was no way that she could have just one taste, one night with this man and not leave with her mind forever wondering about him. He was just too entrancing, too alluring for her to not to be drawn to him so strongly. If there was no chance that her heart might become involved she wouldn't have hesitated…but self-preservation was the driving force that kept her from giving in. As much as she wanted him…she had to say no.

Or risk a bruised and regretful heart when she had to leave him with the sunrise.

"I will not disappoint you. I will give you only pleasure, I promise you," he vowed, eyes blazing.

Oh, if only she could believe that! But he had no idea how affected she would be by a sexual encounter with him. She would be forever changed for good or ill. "I'm sorry." Her voice was choked with tears of regret.

Something flared in the depths of his eyes, something dangerous and alarming, and Julia felt a thrill of fear. His eyes glowed fiercely with unchecked emotion and with a lightning quick movement his hands darted out and grabbed her upper arms in a tight grip.

"You have no need to fear me, Julia fair. I know we have only just met...but if you would just take a chance that I will cherish you as you deserve, I promise that you will not be disappointed." He shook her a little then, stunning her with the force of his pent up passion and with his words. "I can turn you inside out with pleasure and you will scream for more, I swear it! You will never know a release like the one I can give you. Trust me to love you and you will never want for anything in my arms."

"Let go of me!" she commanded both alarmed and aroused by his display.

"You do not understand...let me show you." He breathed the last against her lips a second before he brushed them with his.

He had the softest, silkiest lips, full of magic and wonder. She'd known just by looking at them that they had been made for kissing, but she hadn't guessed how perfectly molded and shaped they were—they fit hers as if they had been tailor made. He tasted sweet and spicy all at once, completely and wholly male. Despite his obvious state of turmoil he didn't ravage her mouth—*that* she might have been able to resist, to fight against—instead, he savored and teased, titillated and aroused until she went limp against him and let him have his way.

Gentle pressing gave way to teasing nibbles and Julia was helpless to keep her arms from rising and twining around his strong neck. The feel of his hair was a temptation all its own, pure satin softness that begged her to bury her hands deep within it, which she did immediately. His muscles moved against her, a seductive ripple that seemed both strange and wondrous at the same time, and they were pressed together in the embrace. Nikolai's hands moved from her arms to gently cup the sides of her head as he turned her just so, the better to deepen his kiss.

A tentative lick with his lips was all the warning she was given before he delved deeper. He kissed her as if he wished to devour her whole, as if he would feast on her mouth as he'd feasted earlier on his evening meal. His tongue stroked deeply into her mouth, filling her with the taste of him. She sighed, caught in a glowing, blissful state and he swallowed her breath as if it were his due. He growled against her, vibrating her already swollen lips into tingling life.

His hands became more urgent, more demanding. They speared into her hair, loosening it from its confinement then moved down her back where they fisted at the base of her spine. Julia could only let out a small squeak around Nikolai's still roving mouth as he lifted her against him so that her feet dangled inches off of the floor. He kept her anchored to him effortlessly with an impressive display of strength and Julia fairly swooned with excitement. Against her better judgment she began to lose herself more fully in the embrace.

She kissed him back with all the pent up passion she'd kept contained over the years. Where before he had been the aggressor, now she took command of the kiss. When his thrusting tongue withdrew from her mouth, hers followed it to delve into the sweet spice of his. Their tongues tangled, in a dueling dance of pure eroticism, and they both moaned in response. Her hands roved over the broad planes of his back, reveling in the feel of his rippling muscles beneath the loose fit of his clothing.

Nikolai's fists clutched ever more tightly at her back and he took a small step towards the chair she'd just vacated. He placed one foot on the seat cushion, bringing his knee up between her dangling legs. Julia gasped against his mouth and made to pull away, but now that her weight rested on his bent knee, Nikolai's hands were once again free to move. He anchored her lips against his with a hand at her jaw, keeping her from moving her head more than a few precious inches. His other hand moved down to cup and squeeze the flesh of her buttock, causing her to undulate instinctively against the strong column of his thigh. Warm, liquid desire pooled between her legs almost immediately and she clutched at him in desperation to ride out the storm of feeling that swept through her.

Nikolai's hand remained at her jaw, gently but firmly holding her captive, and his lips strayed from hers after what seemed like an eternity of deep, drugging kisses. Slowly, leisurely, he trailed his mouth from hers, down over the jut of her chin and onto her throat. He nuzzled against her there, pressing tiny warm kisses into the slope of her neck until she let her head fall back boneless and weak. Julia heard his ragged breathing as he inhaled deeply of her scent. He seemed to enjoy the smell and taste of her, if his broken moan was any sort of indication.

"Julia, my Julia," he breathed against her skin. His hands clenched and then he lifted her away from him. She could have screamed with disappointment at having all that hard, hot male muscle and sinew taken away from her wandering hands but that was before she saw what he meant to do next.

Nikolai set her upon her feet, careful to steady her when she would have fallen on her weak knees. Then he bent over her, never moving his face from the hollow of her throat, growling and murmuring incoherently in his native tongue. His hands moved to the buttons of her blouse and in a surprisingly few short seconds he had bared her from neck to navel. All that remained was the coral pink bra, a last barrier between them. His hands wandered, stroking over the soft flesh of her belly, and his face lowered into the valley between her breasts where he suddenly stilled, breathing deep.

In a graceful motion that startled her—it was too fluid for a man of his mass and stature—he knelt before her. Even in her drunken arousal Julia could see how his hands trembled when they rose to cup the heavy weight of her breasts. He held her gently, carefully, as if he feared she might break, and she felt the soft press of his mouth on one of her covered nipples.

She moaned and marveled that the broken sound had actually come from her own mouth. Her knees were shaking and her panties were soaked through with the evidence of her fierce arousal. She'd never before felt so awakened to passion, so ready for that next step in the mating dance between male and female.

Nikolai's mouth drew her attention once more as he moved it down, nuzzling into that hollow beneath her breasts. She felt the gentle bite of his teeth and then the immediate lave of his tongue, which eased the tiny sting. He moved further down, sitting low on his knees now, and buried his face against the fleshy softness of her belly. There came again that deep, rumbling growl from within his chest and throat. It sounded too animalistic and far too dangerous to belong to a human throat and would have alarmed her had she not been so caught up in the heat of the moment. He buried his face more deeply against her, clutching at her almost desperately, and snarled yet again.

With a flurry of motion he shoved away from her, sending her teetering. In the blink of an eye he had put the distance of the balcony between them, burying himself deep within the shadows so that she could no longer see him clearly.

"Go, Julia. You have your reprieve for tonight." His voice was guttural and heavily accented now, completely changed in cadence and tone from the clear, musical quality he'd displayed throughout the night. The sound was unnerving in the extreme and the sense of fear which had been with her at different times throughout the night, came back with a roar of warning through her system.

With trembling hands she clumsily righted her clothing, not knowing how to respond to Nikolai's sudden change of mood. She seemed to be taking too long for Nikolai snarled again and almost roared his last words.

"*Go now, woman*! You wanted to leave, now do so. For pity's sake, right your clothing once you're safe in the hall corridor." His voice choked off into silence, leaving his words to echo between them.

Julia felt her temper soar at his words. How dare he bark commands at her like she was some kind of servant! He was the one who had pursued her after her initial withdrawal. He was the one who had swept her up into an embrace that had stolen away her senses and made her yearn for more, not the other way around.

"Fine, I'll go. It *is* what I want, anyway," she lied. "Next time don't pretend to be so frickin' eager when its obvious that you're not." She marched off of the balcony and headed through the suite to the door. It was dark in the rooms. Nikolai must have snuffed out all but the bedroom light—which had served to illuminate their dinner on the balcony—when he'd gone to accept their room service tray.

"*Ebat'-kopat'*! Is that what you think? That I pretended to want you?"

Julia jumped with a muffled shriek. Nikolai had said the words right at her ear, but she hadn't even known he was following her, much less following her so closely. She whirled and regarded his shadowy form with a frown.

"I'm not going to pursue this conversation further. You've made your intentions known, now that you've seen me half naked—which I'm sure was a big disappointment for you—it's obvious you want nothing more to do with me." She spoke so quickly that her words tripped, one over the other. She was embarrassed as never before and suddenly grateful for the darkness that helped to hide her blush of shame. She felt the pain of his rejection like a knife through her heart, but was thankful, at least, that he'd rejected her *before* he'd slept with her.

"I will not dignify your nonsensical ramblings beyond stating that you are even more beautiful 'half naked' than I could have imagined. But you have to go. I feel...sick...all of a sudden. I was so harsh with you because I did not want you to see me disgrace myself after so perfect an evening."

He sounded so honest, so believable that her heart immediately softened with sympathy. "Was it something you ate? Do you need any medicine? Should you lay down?"

"Perhaps it was the food. I do not know. Please Julia, go before I make an even bigger ass of myself. I am sorry if I spoiled your evening. I am sorry if I scared you. Can I see you tomorrow night after work?"

Julia thought about it and nodded before she even knew she meant to. Then she remembered how dark it was and made to speak, but Nikolai put a hand at her back, opened the door for her and gently moved her through it.

"I will see you tomorrow night, then. Sleep well, Julia fair."

The door closed firmly behind her before she could answer and she exhaled, exasperated at how the evening had turned out. She would never understand men as long as she lived. They were so confusing!

It took her a few minutes to make her way to the reception area where she gathered her sketchbook and purse and called a cab to come and pick her up. Luckily Nora was off somewhere for the moment so she wasn't waylaid by a thousand and one questions regarding her date. Inexplicably a lump rose to her throat at the thought of going home to her empty apartment, but she quickly turned her thoughts to happier ones. She'd just had a wonderful dinner—without having to pay for it—and been kissed by the sexiest man she'd ever met. What more could a girl want, now really?

Julia walked out to her rented cab, head bowed against the sudden bite of the wind that whipped her hair about as it swept down between the tall buildings that surrounded her. As she stepped into the cab, in the moment before she closed the door and the driver started the engine, she could have sworn she heard a sound that had no business being in the sterile confines of the city.

The long and mournful wail of a wolf.

Chapter Five

ꟽ

Nikolai gripped the railing of his balcony and let out another mournful cry to the heavens. He had seen Julia as she'd stepped into the yellow car and been driven away. Away from him. It had taken all of his self-control to keep from begging her to stay, from crying out her name in desperation when he had spotted her down below. It had torn apart his insides to see her leave him…but he'd had no choice but to push her away.

Something wasn't quite…*right*…inside of him.

Nikolai looked up into the sky, his sharp eyes easily picking out the shape of the moon despite the coverage of a sudden gathering of clouds before it. The moon was still a sliver in the night sky, and though it was growing—waxing—it shouldn't be calling to the animal inside of him so strongly yet. But it was, inexplicably enough. He could feel his bones growing and reshaping in his skin. He could feel his muscle and sinew contorting to allow for the change to take him in a sudden rush of strength and power. He could feel the voracious hunger that was always present when his body was ready for the wolf to come forth from within him and take over.

But it was too early! It was far too soon in the moon's phasing for the final change into his wolf.

For him, losing control was an unforgivable sin. He'd come so close to…his thoughts faltered at that. What had he come close to doing? Eating her? *No,* he immediately turned away from that repugnant thought. Ravaging her? No, never that. But when he'd been on his knees before her, scenting the sultry sweet feminine softness that was weeping for him between her legs, he'd almost *bitten* her! His jaws had ached with the need to sink his sharpening teeth into her soft, downy flesh. He hadn't wanted to hurt her…never that. But the urge to bite was a dangerous one, one that had struck fear in his heart for her continued safety with him. He'd doubted his own will, his own self-control.

How could she ever forgive him? How could he ever forgive himself?

But when he'd apologized—explained that he wasn't feeling well—Julia had immediately let go of her anger with him. She'd cared for his welfare, even after his unforgivable treatment of her but moments before. His mate was far more softhearted and understanding than he would have been under the same circumstances. He knew that he'd hurt her tender feelings. Knew that she'd wanted him as desperately as he'd wanted her, but she had still agreed to meet him the very next night. Surely he was the luckiest being on Earth tonight.

Julia. His mate. What a lovely thought that was. How sweet the words sounded when he whispered them into the night wind. He'd waited so long, been alone and solitary for so many years. Now, to find his one—his only—amongst humans, in a city halfway across the globe, it was a shock and a surprise. But at least he now knew why his visions and dreams had driven him to come to this cold, forbidding city. His instincts had been alerted to her existence, even at such a grand distance, and led him here to find her.

His cousin, Ivan, was the first and only of their kind to ever mate with a human female. And his mate, Brianna, had come to him, not the other way around. Ivan had not sensed his mate until she'd stepped foot on their native soil. But Nikolai was an alpha male, the pack's Bodark, their leader by right of strength and cunning. His powers were far more potent and so he had sensed Julia's existence, even across a vast ocean that separated them. He cringed when he remembered how long he'd been ignoring his visions. How many years had gone by since the first dream had begun urging him to leave his homeland? Three? Four? And perhaps the most important question of all, the one that might shed a bit of light on the issue…just how long had Julia lived in New York?

Nikolai's skin rippled and he gasped, gritting his teeth. One of his fangs cut into his lower lip, drawing blood. It was too soon! True, the moon was waxing, calling forth his more animalistic instincts. He already noticed that his body was gaining in musculature and strength. He was growing surlier in demeanor when around the humans of the city. He was hungry for the juiciest, bloodiest cuts of meat. His hair and nails were growing ever faster. His movements were gaining in speed and grace, as they always did during this time of the month, but it was far too soon for his bones to crack and reshape, for his muscles to shudder and ripple, and for his full fangs to show. And his eyes, always brighter than those of humans, were glowing bright enough to illuminate objects but a few feet away, much like a flashlight or torch, something that only happened in the last days before the full moon.

If only he could hold off the change for a little longer. Long enough to woo his mate into coming with him when he returned to his native land. And he would have to return, very soon. Nikolai had no idea what he would do if he were forced to become a wolf within the city limits. Someone might get hurt. He might get hurt. He might go insane, being so confined in a concrete prison such as this New York was turning out to be. He'd never heard of others like him meeting the full moon outside of their borders, or within a city even half so big as this. Perhaps it wasn't possible. Or perhaps this was the very reason why he was so out of sorts with himself now. Perhaps the city forced the change on his kind if they stayed too long.

He needed to leave and leave soon. But the thought of leaving Julia was abhorrent to him. She had to come with him. She was his mate and she belonged by his side. Surely she would see that and agree to come home with him. True, she was a human and unknowing of the tie that bound them together, but her heart could not long deny his no matter how stubborn she was. Julia would have to come with him. It was the only way.

And heaven help her if she chose to deny them…because he could not.

Chapter Six

ꟸ

"You are mine, Julia. You know that, don't you?" His voice sent shivers of raw need racing through her. "You've always been mine."

"Yes, yours. Always yours." She moaned.

Julia opened her eyes to see Nikolai's icy blue orbs shining down at her from the dark shadows of her room. His form was stretched out, lying full upon her beneath the coverlet on her bed and the heavy evidence of his arousal was nestled between her already quivering thighs. Julia couldn't help but move beneath him, undulating in such a way that she cuddled the fierce, hard column of strength that prodded at her most secret place.

Julia moaned then as he lowered his lips and found her nipple. His mouth was hot as flame on her sensitive flesh and she felt the textured scrape of his tongue as he licked over her puckered areole. Her breath came in short, desperate pants as his teeth and tongue worked on her and that, coupled with the exquisite sensation of his free hand kneading the fullness of her other breast was almost enough to make her come undone completely. He sucked harder on her, as if sensing her desperate need, and she moaned again, raggedly.

Endless, colored lights danced about in her mind, like a splintered rainbow behind her eyes. Delicious, liquid pleasure raced through her from head to toe and she bucked under his weight in response. She felt the heat of his desire roll off of him in waves and heard him murmur deeply in response to her impassioned movements. Fire pooled low in her belly and caused a flood of moisture to rush between her legs. Her thighs opened with a will of their own and Nikolai immediately settled between them. The velvet steel of his phallus rubbed deliciously against her weeping slit and he growled low in his throat, vibrating the nipple in his mouth until the pleasure of it became a torture that was almost more than she could bear.

There came a desperate cry and, too late, Julia realized it was she who made the sound. She quaked and moaned beneath his weight, feeling both cherished and dominated as his mouth and hands stroked over her body. She strained upwards against him, firmly locking her legs around his waist, and felt his cock slide fully against the wet valley between her legs. She felt the tip of him just enter her and braced herself for his next move, but he immediately stilled the smooth glide of his flesh into hers. His hands petted over her, soothing her fevered skin, but his mouth moved to her other nipple to lick and suckle her, driving her up to wild heights once again.

He murmured in that deliciously wicked and sensual voice of his, something in Russian that made her moan, even though she couldn't understand it. His hands moved around her body to squeeze and separate her buttocks and his erection rubbed back and forth against her wet, swollen flesh. He pulled her tight against him and they both groaned. With her legs spread wide around his middle, Nikolai easily moved in a slip slide dance against her center. She could feel the gentle scrape of his pubic hair against her, rocking over her clit until it was engorged and screaming for more of the sweet torment. Without entering her, he thrust and withdrew against her in such a way that her entire labia was stoked to weeping life. The wet welcome of her body aided in his movements against her but even as she teetered on the brink of orgasm she knew it wasn't enough.

She wanted him to fill her, to *take* her. Only then would she be truly sated.

In a burst of frustrated energy she rolled them over so that she held the dominant position in the bed. With a satisfied sigh she began to sink down over his thick cock, her channel flooded anew with a rush of silken wetness to better ease his way. The great plumed head of his penis slipped into her, stretching her so fully that she gasped and dug her nails into the firm muscles of his chest. She felt the blood pulse through his shaft like a tiny fist and then her vagina clenched with her first, blessed tremors of release.

"Yes! Yes, *oooooo*," she cried out helplessly.

Just as she felt his cock slide deeper into her, Nikolai reversed their positions again, pinned her hands to the bed and rose over her. His wintry eyes bore down into hers and suddenly he seemed a terrifying vision of more than just a mere man. Something dangerous swam in his eyes, something dark and mysterious, in a look that she couldn't possibly hope to understand. Julia tried to look away but before she could Nikolai lowered his forehead to hers and kept her gaze locked to his with only the force of his will. In that moment he was pure dominating male and it pushed her over that razor's edge of pleasure into a world of exquisite ecstasy the likes of which she'd never even dreamed.

She bucked wildly against him, her climax splintering like shards of glass through her system, pain and pleasure combined as one. Nikolai reared back, opened his mouth around massive, gleaming fangs, and struck. His teeth sank deep into her breast, drawing blood. But he didn't hurt or maul her and she felt no fear. Only wondrous delight. She screamed, a desperate sound, long and loud and wild, a sound that vaguely reminded Julia of her shrieking morning alarm clock.

Alarm clock...Julia bucked beneath Nikolai's weight, savoring that last deep thrust...that last deep bite...

And woke up, moaning and thrashing, alone in her empty bed.

"Damn it! I didn't even finish all the way," Julia griped. She rolled over and hit the off button on her alarm clock then sighed and flopped bonelessly once again onto her back. Her body felt swollen and frustrated, still affected by the deliciously sexy events in her dream. She sat up, ran a hand through her tangled hair, and felt a smooth rush of moisture flood out from between her legs, soaking her underwear. She swore again and rose.

"I needed a shower anyway," she muttered.

Not surprisingly, when she turned on the faucet in her shower stall, there was no hot water left for her to bathe in. There rarely was if she didn't rise before six a.m. The tenants of the old apartment building shared one hot water tank which was reportedly just as old as the building itself. So Julia gritted her teeth and stepped beneath the icy spray, shampooing her hair and shaving her legs in record time. When she stepped out of the tiny stall her teeth were chattering and her body was sore from the cold.

"If I were rich I'd take two hour baths in steaming hot water every day," she said, repeating the same mantra she'd been using ever since her first day in the dingy, efficiency apartment. As she dried herself she tried to imagine how warm she would be after such a bath, how rosy and flushed her skin would look, instead of pale and blue and goose pimpled. And instead of the worn scratch of the old towel scraping over her skin now, she imagined the feel of a plush, cushy terry cloth bath towel wrapping her in cozy comfort. She sighed and smiled, imagining how nice it would be to afford new towels willy-nilly whenever the mood struck her. Oh, how decadent was the thought!

Reality intruded, as it was often wont to do and Julia groaned. Today was Saturday, a day often reserved for eating ice cream, watching cartoons, and catching up on schoolwork. But instead of her normal Saturday routine, she would have to rummage through her closet for a decent dress because tonight she was scheduled to hostess The Living Forest soiree. Julia kept reminding herself how much money she was apt to make and thankfully that eased her sour mood a bit. She threw on her favorite worn pair of sweats and went hunting for some decent party clothes.

What a way to start the day, she thought with a grimace.

* * * * *

Julia's face felt like it would freeze in the polite smile she'd been wearing for the past hour. She handed two flutes of champagne to a gentleman in a black tuxedo and turned to pour some punch for an elderly lady who was dressed to the nines in a pink silk ball gown. Julia felt horribly underdressed in her own simple sheath dress, but at least she knew she stood out as part of the "help" in case anyone should need anything. The guests at the party seemed to be a nice bunch of people, for which she was grateful. She'd barely left her post behind the bar all night—The Living Forest personnel really enjoyed having their drinks refilled again and again.

For what seemed the hundredth time that night she had the discomfiting sense of being watched and whipped her head around to see who might be staring at her. As far as she could tell there was no one looking at her, but she could have sworn that someone was watching her again. She was starting to feel positively paranoid. Perhaps she was just over tired. Admittedly her night had been a long one and then she'd awakened at her usual morning hour to prepare for the day. She hadn't slept but a few short hours.

"You look a little lost."

Julia started at the deep voice that broke over her musings and turned to look at the speaker. Her polite smile faltered from her lips when she locked eyes with the darkest chocolate orbs she'd ever seen. The man before her was shockingly handsome and quite obviously, exotically, of Native American decent. He had high cheekbones, a hawkish nose over sensually sculpted lips, and long ebony hair that shone like glass down his back. Even in his stylish evening attire he had about him a mysterious aura that pulled at her in the strangest of ways.

Aside from Nikolai, he was probably the most attractive man she'd ever had the pleasure of gawking at.

But that pleasant feeling of spastic butterflies flapping in her stomach never happened, thankfully, and she was able to address him without stuttering. "No, not lost. Just a little tired." She regained her polite smile.

"Well anyone would be tired after having to cater to this bunch. We're known for our long parties. I'm Adrian Darkwood, by the way." He offered his hand to her across the bar.

"It's nice to meet you Mr. Darkwood. I'm Julia Thurman." She took his hand and was surprised when he didn't shake it. He kissed it gallantly instead.

"Please, call me Adrian. So, I see you've attracted the attention of our guest of honor this evening."

Julia frowned. His words were spoken innocently enough but she sensed a deeper current running beneath them. "I'm not sure what you mean," she said, unable to think of a better response.

"Nikolai Tamits. He's been staring at you all evening." The man chuckled.

"Nikolai? Where? I didn't know he was with your group."

"So you've met him?"

Julia faltered for a moment. Why was this man so interested? She replied with caution, not knowing why she felt a sudden hint of danger flare deep within her. "Well…I work here in the hotel. I've met him, yes, briefly. He seems like a nice gentleman."

"Oh he is, let me assure you. And I'm sorry if I'm alarming you." He gave a short, light laugh. "I have to admit I'm a bit of a matchmaker and I can see that there's something flaring between the two of you. I came over with the intent to introduce the two of you, but I can see that I don't need to bother."

"Where is he? I haven't seen him tonight."

"Just there, by the lobby doors. He keeps moving so you don't see him when you happen to look up." Adrian gave a jaunty wave and Julia followed it with her eyes.

A shiver of sensual awareness raced down her spine when her eyes stumbled into the intense icy-blue fire of Nikolai's gaze. Nikolai looked dangerous and sexy in his tailored tux and the look on his face sent her skin to tingling. He looked as though he wanted to eat her up. Julia smiled at him weakly but he didn't return her shy greeting. Instead his burning eyes strayed from her to the man before her and the look on his face darkened considerably. For some reason Julia couldn't explain she felt guilty that she was talking to Adrian, as if by doing so she was being disloyal to Nikolai, though that didn't make much sense to her befuddled mind.

Adrian drew her attention once more, no small feat when Nikolai was still but a room's distance away.

When he spoke his voice seemed to reverberate in her mind and a compulsion to remember everything he said for future reference overcame a sudden, inexplicable fear of him. "Listen to me now, Julia, and listen well. There will come a time when you'll need answers to questions that are only just now forming in your mind. When that time comes you will seek me out and I will give you those answers. I'll be at The Living Forest personnel offices and I will be expecting you."

His voice changed back to its normal timbre. "Now, may I have some champagne Ms. Thurman?"

Julia felt as though she were coming out of a deep fog. What the hell had he meant by that cryptic warning? Oh well, he was probably having fun at her expense, playing out a joke she didn't understand. She handed him the flute of champagne, hoping he would leave her alone afterward.

"If you'll excuse us Darkwood. Julia and I need to speak privately." Nikolai's voice broke over her nervous thoughts like a calming breeze.

"Of course Mr. Tamits." Adrian turned towards her once again, his eyes boring into hers. "Remember what I said, Ms. Thurman."

Julia nodded politely and gave a sigh of relief when he turned and left.

"What did he say to you?" Nikolai demanded of her, though he still watched the other man's retreating back as he was swallowed into the crowd.

Julia was taken aback by the harsh tone of his words. "I…I don't remember," she lied. She didn't want to repeat Adrian Darkwood's strange warning just now. Nikolai looked to be in too volatile of a temper to hear it anyway. "It wasn't important. Just idle chitchat." She paused, then took the plunge, asking airily, as if it didn't matter, "Why so interested?"

Nikolai turned back to her, stunning her a little with the intense look in his eyes. "I am interested in everything that has to do with you, Julia. Especially where other men are concerned."

Julia had no idea how to respond to that and didn't even begin to try. Instead she turned and served some sodas to a couple that had approached the bar, thankful for the intrusion. But the couple left them alone again, in what seemed record time, thanks to Nikolai's hard stare in their direction. Luckily, though, she didn't have to come up with a response to his impassioned words.

"I have to see you tonight."

"You're seeing me now," Julia quipped with a smile.

"You know what I mean." His voice lowered intimately. "You promised to show me some of your artwork. Show me tonight. After the party."

Julia felt a thrill of pleasure race through her at the thought of being alone with him again. Then felt her heart plummet when she remembered how dingy and poor her apartment would look to him after the splendor of his hotel room.

"I...I don't think you'll be all that interested in my work. Maybe some other time—"

"Tonight. You will take me home with you tonight..." His voice was compelling.

Julia grew inexplicably lightheaded and heard herself speak before she had time to think on the words. "Okay. I just have to stay until the party is over, then we can go."

"I will have the company limo wait for us outside. You will not run from me, Julia."

Julia felt like she was swimming in a dream when she answered him, but she couldn't have denied him had her life depended on it. "I won't run," she answered, knowing her voice sounded heavy. Drugged. Perhaps she was more tired than she'd thought. The night was growing more and more surreal for her.

"Until later then, my love." His voice held a dangerous promise that, even in her dreamy state, Julia couldn't ignore.

Until later, indeed, she thought as he stalked gracefully away from her. What arrogance! She sighed, shook her head to clear it and pasted her polite smile back on her face. It was going to be a long night.

* * * * *

Julia felt Nikolai's strong hand at the small of her back as he led her out to the long, black stretch limousine that awaited them in front of the hotel. Nikolai paused to look up at the sky and Julia saw him shudder once, before he looked away and opened the door to the vehicle for her. When they were seated next to each other, after Julia had given their driver her address, Nikolai erected the privacy shield between them and their chauffeur. Then he turned to take her chin gently in his hand, locking his gaze to hers.

"You will not fear me, Julia. I would never willingly hurt you, so you have no need to fear when I am near you." His voice was an echo that played over and over in her mind and before she knew it many minutes had passed and they were already on their way to her home.

After that Julia felt like two different people as she sat next to Nikolai. One person was confused, disoriented, and unable to speak or move within her own skin. Trapped behind a wall from which there was no escape, unless her escort should will it. The other person...well, she was someone totally alien to Julia. This person laughed and reveled wantonly in the attentions of the powerfully magnetic man at her side. This other person seemed content to let Nikolai lead them on a dangerous journey that would end only heaven knew where. This other person was just as dangerous to Julia as Nikolai himself was.

Julia felt a strong compulsion riding her, the need to touch and be touched by her escort. It wasn't purely a sexual urge, though that was indeed strong within her. It was as though she couldn't feel at all comfortable or safe, unless some part of her was in constant contact with Nikolai. So as they reclined in the luxurious back seat of the limousine, Julia turned to him and rubbed her body in a shamelessly sensual, feline movement against his.

Nikolai turned to her and, in kind, rubbed the entire length of his body against hers. At the end of his shifting movement, he positioned them so that she lay stretched out beneath him as much as the seat would allow. A low, dangerous snarl poured out from his lips and Julia saw the flash of sharp, gleaming teeth. He writhed against her again and bent to nip at the flesh of her neck.

His lips and teeth nibbled their way up to her gasping mouth. Nikolai pulled back to meet her eyes with his, and that buried part of Julia moaned in arousal to see his icy blue eyes blazing with deadly intent down into hers. Then, with a swift and striking movement, Nikolai laid his lips to hers, burning and searing them with the intensity of his kiss. Neither of Julia's selves could hope to resist such a potent and erotic lure as he brought them more deeply into the kiss. With a breathy sigh, she surrendered herself completely to him and returned his ardor with full enthusiasm.

Julia moaned as his velvet tongue delved between the seam of her lips. He captured the sound with his mouth before sensuously licking at the roof of her mouth in reward. His tongue delved deep, imitating the thrust and withdraw of an even more intimate love play. His lips slanted over hers in such a way that she knew he would not stop until he had tasted all she had to offer. Julia could not resist joining her tongue in the mating dance, tasting his wild flavor, savoring every moment of the delicious exploration.

Their bodies writhed and strained against one another as they kissed. Nikolai's hair tickled her face and shoulders as they moved, caressing her like a thousands teasing hands. His hands were clutched desperately at her hips, moving her against him in such a way that she had no doubts as to the extent of his desire for her. She felt his nails dig into her flesh and gasped at the pleasure-pain that radiated through her from the small wounds.

Immediately his hold on her eased and he allowed his hands to rove freely over her body. The sensations of his touch, even through her dress, made her flesh sing and strain for more of him. His hands spread wide, seeking to cover every possible inch of her that he could manage. He ran his hands down her waist, to her thighs and calves, then up to her ribs and finally to her breasts. There his hands lingered, gently cupping her flesh like a precious flower, even as his mouth continued to ravage hers.

Julia moaned in ecstasy, feeling her body climb that endless peak towards release. The sound seemed to awaken something feral within Nikolai, for suddenly his hands and mouth were everywhere all at once. He growled and nipped at her with his teeth, he licked and laved at her breasts through the fabric of her dress. His hands clutched and gripped at her, racing over her, tugging at the impediment of her clothing.

The bodice of her sheath dress was too tightly laced against her for Nikolai to merely push aside the material, though he tried. Making an impatient sound, he tore at the barrier that kept her breasts covered from his gaze. Cloth ripped, a loud sound in the confines of the limousine, and then at last she was bared to his hungry eyes. Nikolai suddenly paused and pulled back from her, even as she strained to draw him closer.

His blue eyes were hot as flame as he drank her in with his gaze. "You are so beautiful. I never knew…I never dreamed that such sweet perfection could exist." His voice was strained and his Russian accent was even more pronounced than usual as he spoke.

His eyes rose to meet hers and no further words were needed between them. He kept his gaze locked to hers as he slowly, oh so slowly, lowered his head to her naked breast. His tongue darted out and lightly licked at one puffed up nipple, causing it to stiffen and harden even further as it strained of its own volition for more of his attention. His thick, heavy lashes shuttered his gaze and he sighed, the warmth of his breath acting as a caress all its own. Then he drew her nipple into his mouth, savoring it like a sweetly sugared candy.

"*God,*" Julia gasped and her body bowed beneath him, only to be soothed again by his roaming hands. Electric fire danced from where his mouth fed at her nipple straight down to her curling toes. Her blood thundered in her ears and her breaths sounded out in desperate, moaning pants. Never before had she felt such need, such endless hunger for another person, as she did then. "*Oh, God,*" she rasped out again.

Nikolai pulled back and grinned—a dangerous flash of blazing white teeth. "I would be your god, my Julia. And your worshipping slave for all the rest of our days, if you would but give yourself to me freely."

"*I do,*" she moaned shamelessly. "I am yours, only yours. Do with me what you will." Her body moved against his in such a way that her heated core rubbed fully, erotically, against his straining cock.

His hands clenched in a spasm against her. He let out a soft, keening howl and took her mouth once more in his. He kissed her with such ferocity, such mindless and heated abandon, that Julia felt his teeth bite into the tender flesh of her lip and she tasted her own blood.

With a great anguished roar Nikolai flung himself violently from her, coming to rest in the seat opposite to the one on which Julia still lay. The luxurious cab of the limousine seemed suddenly far too small for the two of them. Nikolai was a wild and caged beast in his passionate retreat. Dangerous. Deadly.

"Why did you stop?" she wailed.

Nikolai snarled low, softly, in his throat. When he answered her, his voice was rough and deep. "We will continue this in the privacy of your home. I will not take you this first time in the back of a metal box."

Julia's two selves shimmered and became whole again and she gasped. She'd almost given up her virginity in the backseat of a limo! That was definitely not how she'd envisioned her deflowering. So she nodded shakily in agreement and righted her clothing as best she could.

"Here, take this, love." Nikolai offered her his tuxedo jacket, which she donned thankfully.

Julia looked out of the window at the scenery as they sped by and realized how close they were to her house. She turned to see Nikolai's eyes burning out at her from the shadowy confines of the vehicle's dark interior.

She sighed, realizing the moment of truth was upon them. "My apartment…it's not…well, it's kind of small." Hearing her own words, she cringed. She sounded like a half-wit. "It's not what you would call…luxurious by any means—"

"I promise you that I do not care about any of that, Julia." He brushed her words away.

"No, you don't understand. The building I live in is old and not—"

Nikolai moved to take her hands in his and it was then that she realized they were trembling. Whether with remembered passion or nervousness she couldn't say because she felt both emotions strongly. "I do not care how you live, Julia. I know you are not rich and I know you work hard to make ends meet, but that is only a small part of who you are and it is nothing to be ashamed of."

"But you're obviously well off," she faltered.

"Why should that matter? I have some money, yes, enough to live comfortably on in your city. But I have no need of that where I come from and shamefully I did not earn it, I inherited it—as my parents inherited it and so forth—from long years of investing. I do not live in rich surroundings; I live in a log cabin deep in the woods. I have no electricity—there is none to be had so secluded is my village—and there are no shops nearby. My people and I, we live off of our lands. We hunt for our meat and grow our own vegetables. To many outsiders, this lifestyle would seem poor and uncomfortable, but it is not. It is full of happiness and smiles and joy. I would not trade it for a dozen lifetimes spent in your luxurious hotel."

"Oh. Well, in that case...we're almost there." She offered him a wane smile.

Nikolai held her hand in his, fingers entwined in hers. "I cannot wait," he said with a wolfish grin.

Chapter Seven

ℬ

Nikolai seemed to swallow up the small living room with his size but he didn't comment on it, and Julia was grateful to him for it. She saw his eyes flare when they took in the décor of her home—when he saw the paintings and drawings that crowded her walls, and the sculptures of various shapes and sizes that dotted the shelves and niches of the room—and was pleased with his reaction. For her, the night was turning out to be full of surprises.

Nikolai muttered something in Russian and ran an unsteady hand through his golden hair, tousling it. "*Ebat'-kopat'!*" There came again that exclamation he used, one she was already swiftly becoming familiar with. "You created all of these?" He swept his hand out to encompass the whole of the room.

Julia felt her cheeks stain with a blush. Oh yes, she was certainly pleased with his reaction. "Yeah. The landscapes are the newest—they're still drying—and the portraits are from several years ago, when I still lived with my parents."

"They are remarkable," he said with a look of surprise.

Julia laughed. "Most people don't remark on it too much when I *say* I'm an artist, but when they see my work they treat me a little more seriously. My professors say it'll only get worse as I gain in skill and popularity."

"Certainly." Nikolai cleared his throat and for the first time Julia saw him grow awkward. "I expected you to be good, of course I did, but this…I have never seen more realistic work. Your portraits are excellent, like photos come to life. And the colors you use for your landscapes…they are so vivid, so different from what I am used to seeing on canvas. Not that I am an expert but…" he faltered.

"You know what you like? I've heard that too many times to count. Everyone's a critic whether they try to be or not." Julia smiled. "But I thank you for the compliments. I'm glad you like my work."

"Why are you going to school? You do not need further training, surely."

"Thanks for that vote of confidence, but proper training is important. Well, it helps to round out one's skills, anyway. And if I have a degree it will be easier to get a job in the open market, though I'd love to just be a freelancer. But if I can't find work, I can always fall back on a teaching position at the college. It's just smart to get my degree while I can. I have a small scholarship, which pays for most of my classes, so I'm not going to be too deep out of pocket for the experience, so I'm taking advantage of the situation while I can."

Nikolai was silent as he prowled around the room studying her work. It was several minutes later when he turned back to her and the look in his eyes singed her down to her toes.

"It is clear you hide a lot of passion inside of you. Your work reflects the vibrancy of your inner self." He advanced on her, crowding her against a wall with the use of nothing but the sheer mass of his form. "I want to bring that passion to the fore in you, Julia. I want to see you burn for me. And I want you to burn me along with you in the fire that flames between us."

He grabbed her then, fingers digging into her upper arms, and lowered his lips to hers. Julia gasped at the sudden, unexpected movement, allowing his tongue immediate entrance into her mouth. Their teeth met and their lips meshed tightly together. Julia moaned her surprise and he immediately softened the embrace, tracing her lips lightly with his tongue before delving deeper once more. He licked the roof of her mouth and slid his tongue over and around hers, filling her mouth with the wild, exotic taste of him. He sucked her tongue gently into his mouth and she repeated his caresses with some of her own, exploring him as thoroughly as he had explored her.

Nikolai growled into her mouth, a desperate and hungry sound, then pulled away to trail his heated mouth down over her jaw. In a move that reminded her of their first meeting he licked a long path down her jaw and throat to settle over the pulse that beat frantically in her neck. He suckled her there, while his hands roved down from her arms, clutching into fists at her hips and kneading her like a cat. Julia's head fell limply back as he nuzzled her and her knees turned to water. She sagged against him limply and he reached around her, gathering her close.

"You feel so good," he groaned into her throat.

"So do you," she whispered raggedly, throwing her arms around his neck.

"I can smell how much you want me, taste how much you need me. I am trying to go slow but...you make me forget myself." His mouth trailed back up so that he could trace the shell of her ear with his tongue.

Julia could only moan and press hurried, desperate kisses to whatever part of him she could reach—his temple, his hair, his jaw. She was maddened with lust, more aroused than she had ever been before and desperate to have him inside of her. Her entire body tingled from head to toe. Her thighs quaked and shivered, her nipples were hard, tingling points and her vagina felt swollen and achy. She latched onto him, anchoring her arms around him, and crawled up his body like it was a tree. Nikolai steadied her with his hands beneath her bottom and she locked her ankles about his waist, rocking against him shamelessly.

"Calm down, sweet, please. I cannot hold back from you when you move like that," he breathed into her ear, before darting his tongue into it once more.

"I can't calm down. I need you, I really do," she cried out. She didn't understand herself, had never known she could be so wild, so abandoned. But it felt so right to be there in his arms that she couldn't have calmed down had she tried. And she didn't want to try. She wanted only to be with him. In every way. Arching her hips against him again she cuddled the hard column of his erection in the vee of her thighs, rubbing her clit against him until it tingled deliciously.

He thrust against her, then groaned and stilled. He lowered his head to hers, breathing raggedly into her mouth, so that every breath she took was dependent on his exhalation. She moaned and thrashed in his embrace, desperate to find release.

"*Shh*, it is all right." Nikolai adjusted her in his arms so that her center came into full contact with his hardness, spreading her legs ever wider. "Rock against me just like that. Find your release, love. There will be time for slowness afterward. Yes, that is it," he breathed when she began a rhythmic rocking against him. "Ride me. Ride me hard." He helped her motions, lifting and lowering her with strong hands cupping the flesh of her buttocks.

Julia dug her nails into the muscles of his back beneath his shirt. Her ankles rested on his firm, tight buttocks as she moved on him. Her breath came in desperate, moaning pants. She felt her body tightening, tensing in preparation for release...but it wasn't enough. "Please, *please*," she begged, not certain what she was begging for.

But Nikolai needed no explanation. He knew what she wanted, what she needed and craved. In a swift movement that startled Julia, he turned and lowered her to the floor. He pushed up her dress and tore aside her satin panties, cleanly ripping through the fabric. Then, oh blessed relief, his fingers were on her at last. He parted the slick folds of her pussy, spreading them wide, and dipped his fingers into the wet heat of her. Julia cried out and bucked against his hand, spreading her legs out as far as they could go to allow him free access to her most sensitive tissues. His thumb moved up to press and massage the hard nubbin of her clit and he thrust one long, strong finger into the depths of her.

Julia came undone. A wild, warm flood burst over her, taking her under into an ocean of wondrous sensation. She felt the walls of her channel rhythmically gripping the finger that penetrated her, felt a flush suffuse her from head to toe. Her nipples swelled even further and stabbed towards the heavens and Nikolai's gifted thumb continued to manipulate her clit until she was bucking wildly against him, over and over, without a care for propriety. Her back bowed up off of the floor, neatly lodging his finger even more deeply into her until her pleasure mingled with pain and she screamed.

It was several moments later before Julia could think clearly again. She was dizzy, lightheaded, and filled with a deep satisfaction that was unlike anything she'd ever experienced before.

"You are so beautiful when you find release," Nikolai breathed. He shifted her body and before she knew what was happening he had divested her of the last remnants of her clothing. "I need to taste you, Julia. I need to drink from your fount and know that it weeps only for me."

His thick accent rolled over her and the lyrical words made her body tingle anew with desire. She loved the way he spoke to her, as if she were a marvel and a wonder to him.

Nikolai moved down between her legs and it was then that she realized exactly what he wanted to taste. He braced his hands on her inner thighs, gently holding her legs spread wide for him. His hot breath tickled over her trembling vagina, but before he lowered his lips to her he looked up and locked his eyes to hers.

"Watch me when I taste you, Julia. I want you to see me as well as feel me. I want there to be no doubt in your mind that it is me, Nikolai, feasting here between your lovely legs."

Julia's eyes widened at his words and then shuttered as he set his mouth upon her.

His lips were hot as flame. She felt him suckle at her, drinking her up, and saw his head move back and forth as he savored every inch of her. His beautiful eyes closed and his long black lashes made dusky shadows on his cheekbones, but she didn't look away—he had commanded that she watch—she had to watch. She saw him pull back slightly, saw his tongue reach out until it looked indecently long, then felt him lap at her juices. Over and over he licked her, until she was soaking wet with the fluids he coaxed forth from her. He seemed to enjoy the flavor of her, because he drank every last drop she had to give and still rooted for more.

Then his tongue, his long, velvet tongue, entered her like a phallus. He reached depths of her that had never before been reached, seeming to taste her very womb. He moaned against her, vibrating her, and she rocked helplessly against him as he fucked her with his mouth. His tongue thrust in and out of her, filling all of her empty spaces but making her long for an even tighter, fuller penetration. Her hands speared into his golden hair, reveling in the silken texture, and his movements increased in speed and force against her. His mouth made wet, sucking noises against her, and the sounds drove her wild with desire. She moved up against him, mashing his face more deeply into her wet heat, and cried out when his tongue impaled her at a new and altogether delicious angle.

Nikolai pulled back then, squeezed her ass cheeks apart gently, and she saw a long, silver trail of saliva escape his mouth. She felt it splash onto the puckered flesh of her anus just before he lowered his mouth back onto her vagina. But this time, when his tongue speared deep into her, she felt another, delicious penetration down below. Nikolai tenderly slipped his finger into the tight ring of her anus, awakening Julia to new and heretofore unimagined delights. As he sucked and thrust at her pussy, his finger slowly thrust and withdrew in her bottom, making her body shudder with the delicious torments. Unbelievably her body tightened once more, readying itself for another explosive climax.

Julia thrashed on the floor, once, twice, hanging on by a thread…and then his upper lip brushed against her clit and she lost herself in her orgasm. She bore down on the tongue and finger that impaled her, feeling the pulses of release wrack her body until even her scalp tingled with mind-numbing pleasure. "God, yes! Ooooo, yeessss!" she screamed.

When Julia came back to herself once again, Nikolai was lazily lapping up the last of her juices. His tongue laved her all over, leaving no part of her unexplored. Where before his ministrations had driven her mad with lust, they now served to comfort her trembling, swollen tissues. She let him have his way, spread out limply on the floor beneath him with her legs splayed wide. It seemed that he would never tire of licking her. He suckled the folds of her labia, licked deep within her channel with his incredibly long tongue and with his lips, softly kissed every inch of her vagina.

After what seemed like hours Nikolai pressed one last kiss to the crown of her sex then slowly, predatorily crawled up her body until he stared down into her face. He licked his lips lazily, sexily, and sent her a hot look with his shining eyes. "Sweeter than honey, headier than wine. You have intoxicated me…but I want more. I want all of you."

Julia felt a thrill of anticipation. The look in his eyes promised that the night was far from over for both of them. And if this overture were any indication of the delights that awaited her in his arms, the night would be unforgettable.

Chapter Eight

ꟗ

Nikolai lifted her off the floor and cradled her in his arms, no small feat of strength, all without even grunting under the burden of her weight. His nostrils flared as if scenting something on the air, and with uncanny instinct he headed for her bedroom. Of course there were only two doorways that led out of her living room, one went to the bathroom, the other to her bedroom, so he had a fifty-fifty chance of going in the right direction. But it made her happy nonetheless, that he found his way without needing her to guide him. Her brain was—at best—pudding for the moment.

When he entered the darkness of her bedroom he unerringly found his way to her bed and laid her down upon it gently. He kissed her, long and lingeringly so that she tasted herself on his mouth before he pulled away from her once more. From the rustling noises he made Julia realized that he was removing his clothing before he joined her. When he came down upon the bed, the lumpy, worn mattress dipped down beneath his added weight. Nikolai leisurely crawled up over her and hovered for a long, silent moment, eyes positively glowing in the darkness and Julia shuddered with an unexpected thrill of virginal nervousness.

"There will be no going back after this, Julia. For either of us. I want you to know that now, before I go any further." His words were hushed but they affected her with such a force that he could have shouted them at her. It wasn't so much what he said, it was how he said it that surprised her. He sounded as if he meant every word. As if they were a promise...or a threat. The moment was a serious one—a life changing one—but there was never any chance that she would have backed down from this encounter with him. She wanted him. She *needed* him. That was all that mattered to her in that moment.

Her silence seemed to be enough of a response for him. He leaned down and breathed deeply of her scent, then licked his tongue over her trembling, swollen lips with a delicate and teasing flick.

"You are a goddess, Julia, inside and out. Your beauty shines out of your art, out of your voice and out of your form. I never dreamed that I would find a mate—" His words choked off as if he struggled to stem their flow from his own mouth.

"What?" she urged him, in thrall to the sound of his voice.

"Nothing," he breathed, though Julia knew he was lying. He'd almost said something—something he hadn't wanted to let slip—she was sure. But then he took away her deductive reasoning with another soul-searching kiss and she forgot all about pondering his words further.

His taste filled her mouth once more and Julia feared she would forever be addicted to his unique, masculine flavor. He kept himself propped above her with one hand and let the other stray up to her breast. It hovered there, then trailed lightly over the pouting tip of her nipple. Julia breathed deep, reflexively raising her chest towards his teasing hand and he chuckled against her lips. Then his hand brushed once, twice over her nipple before he gave in to her demands and cupped her breast in his large, callused palm. He rolled her nipple between his thumb and forefinger even as he massaged the plump globe, causing her to moan and undulate against him. There was a connection there between her nipple and her clit, a wondrous and fascinating connection, so that with every pinch and tug of his fingers she felt it down below as if he touched her there, too.

Nikolai sucked her lower lip into his mouth and pulled slowly away. With graceful movements he crawled his way down her body until his mouth hovered over her breasts. She could feel the hot, moist tufts of his breath play over her and then he lowered his leonine head and took her nipple into his mouth. The rough, textured scrape of his tongue, coupled with the satiny texture of his lips made her cry out in sudden, shocking pleasure. Her breast ached and her nipple swelled even further in his mouth as he drew on her. She felt the scrape of his teeth and felt a pulse begin to beat deep within her womb in time with his movements against her.

Julia's body bowed up against him and he swept a hand down over her stomach, holding her down with firm but gentle pressure. She groaned and tried to escape his hold, but was unsuccessful. Nikolai took her breast deeper into his mouth and drew on her more forcefully, almost to the point of pain. Mewling in her throat, Julia thrashed her head about and clutched at his wide shoulders. Her fingernails dug into the firm muscles and he groaned against her. She pulled back, fearing that she'd injured him in her ardor.

Nikolai paused in his ministrations at her breast. "Do not stop," he said raggedly, causing his breath to play teasingly over her moistened nipple.

Julia reached for him again as he moved to her other breast, giving it the same attentions as he had the first one. She spread her legs eagerly and he settled between them. His hand still held her practically immobile beneath him, but her legs were now free to move against his lightly furred calves and thighs, which she did with great enthusiasm. Nikolai's teeth scraped against her nipple, hard, causing her to squeal in surprise and rake her nails down his back in retaliation. He yelped like a wounded puppy then chuckled against her and gently kissed away the small pain he'd given her.

Nikolai shook his head back and forth over her, causing his hair to spill heavily onto her heated flesh. He used his hair to tease and torment her until she was crying out over and over with each delightful caress of the thick, silken strands. Moving like a song, fluid and sensual, he rolled his body against her, using it to pet her from neck to toe, leaving no part of her untouched. With each brush of his chest on hers, her nipples shivered and puckered into tight stabbing points. With each movement his body made, his burning rod nudged against her belly and his pubic hair scraped erotically against hers. His sac bounced gently against the swollen and tender flesh between her legs, adding yet another sensation to swamp her senses and drive her wild.

Bending his knees, using them to spread her legs wider apart, he leaned back and inhaled deeply. "You smell like me, now." His voice was guttural, rough and thick, almost unintelligible. Like he was speaking around cotton in his mouth. "And I smell like you. I will never get your scent out of my nostrils, your taste out of my mouth." He made a noise, like a muffled mewl or howl in his throat, and bent at an unbelievable angle from his crouching position, to press his face into her stomach.

His hands moved to her hipbones, biting into the flesh there just short of causing her pain. Julia tangled her hands in his hair and pulled him even closer against her. She felt his teeth bite softly into her once, twice, three times, as if he were testing the resiliency of her skin. He pulled back, lifting her hips with his hands, never moving his face from her tummy, until she was bowed sharply up off of the mattress. Her head dug deeply into the pillow and she gasped. She'd never felt so helpless, so elementally dominated. Nikolai was strong—alarmingly so—but he seemed to know her limits and only manipulated her body as far as it would comfortably go.

Julia gasped in surprise when he neatly flipped her over onto her stomach and came down to whisper into her ear, words which caused her to shiver with a mixture of anticipation and nervousness. "I need you this way our first time, on your hands and knees before me. Hold onto the sheets, as tight as you can, and open yourself to me. Let me claim you...I *need* to claim you. All of you."

His hands positioned her just so, locked and immovable on the frame of her hips. Julia felt the scalding heat of his erection as he rubbed himself against her wetness, making them both slippery with her juices. Nikolai leaned down and licked her from the base of her spine to her shoulder where he hovered, lightly grasping her with his teeth in an elemental and dominant position over her trembling body. Julia felt the head of his cock nudge at her portal, heavy and demanding. Then she felt a pleasurable burning sensation as he stretched her and slowly, inexorably began to fill her up with himself.

His erection was large; she'd known that just from rubbing against him throughout the night. But she was unprepared for just how *large* he really was. He filled her…and filled her…and filled her. And still he came down upon her, the length and breadth of him stealing away her air and making her body tense. The tip of him butted against her virginal membrane deep within her channel—she felt it, knew instinctively that he felt it, too—and then broke through it. Julia cried out with the sudden, pinching pain and then, like a dream, it was gone. Nikolai reared up and roared his satisfaction in a wordless cry.

"Oh Julia, you are well and truly mine. Untouched before. But now claimed." His thick words were arrogant but tender and then he pressed soft, coaxing kisses to her back and shoulders. "Why did you not tell me—warn me? I would have been more gentle," he whispered against her ear.

"I wasn't sure you would notice," she said in a quaking voice.

"I admit I have no experience of such things. But I know enough to recognize a barrier when I feel it. And I can smell your virgin's blood," he admitted ruefully.

How can he smell my blood? I certainly can't smell it.

Julia felt almost faint for a moment with an innate sense that something wasn't quite right with Nikolai, and then lost all rational thought as his cock moved even deeper into her. She hadn't realized until then that he wasn't full seated inside of her yet and this new penetration surprised her into moaning. Nikolai's thick shaft stretched her and filled her with heavy insistence. He moved her on him, bringing her bottom cheeks against the cradle of his thighs, and he was home at last. They groaned in unison.

"You feel…you feel *so* big. *I'm so full,*" she gasped, mindless with the new sensations that swept through her like wildfire.

Nikolai growled and bit into her shoulder again, holding her immobile as he began long, slow thrusts upon her. His cock slipped almost all the way out of her and then sank back inside. Her wet and dripping pussy felt split open as he impaled her over and over, with steady, patient movements. The hands at her hips moved her back against him with each of his forward thrusts, teaching her the rhythm that he set for them both.

The sounds that their bodies made together, moist and earthy, echoed in their ears, spurring them on. The musky perfume of their sex permeated the air of the bedroom, a potent aphrodisiac all its own.

Julia jerked back against him, feeling the walls of her vagina pulse and tighten against his pumping shaft. Nikolai growled and sank his teeth deeper into her shoulder—the better to hold her steady under his weight—and began to thrust harder between her legs. Instinctively sensing that a new angle would give her the deeper penetration that she was coming to crave, Julia lowered her torso onto the mattress and raised her bottom higher against Nikolai's pelvis. The tip of his cock brushed against some hidden button of pleasure inside of her and she keened her appreciation and wonder. The texture of him, velvet on steel, slid against her inner tissues until they were trembling and alive with exquisite sensation, causing her to grow even wetter, even hotter.

Beneath them the bed began to groan and shudder in protest as their movements gained in strength and tempo. Julia felt as if she were racing, hurtling towards her climax. But knew, too, that she would somehow only find release when Nikolai willed it. He was careful to control her every movement, knowingly fine tuning her experience so that she reached heights she'd never before climbed. Her body quaked and shuddered beneath his as she strained more and more towards fulfillment.

"Please, *Nikolai, please,*" she begged, wriggling against his thrusting cock.

Her words turned to keening, desperate cries as he brought her slamming back against him. His movements became ferocious, as he thrust ever deeper, harder, and faster into her eager body.

"Yes, *yeeesssss*!" She muffled a shriek, biting into her pillow.

"*Grrrrrrrrr…*" Nikolai's guttural, satisfied purr vibrated her entire body.

Julia screamed again as Nikolai began to rotate his hips against her, undulating his phallus inside of her in a delicious new dance of erotic savagery. He bit deeper into her shoulder then ripped himself away just before he broke her skin. That pain, coupled with the pleasure of having him fill her so sweetly, brought her at last. Her vagina clenched like a fist down on Nikolai's cock, trembling upon him, taking him along with her into the stars.

They cried out their pleasure as one. Nikolai's hands clenched into fists about her hips as he held her tight to him and pumped her full of his cream. Julia's body accepted every fiery burst that jetted into her, and squeezed and milked for more, ever hungry for all he had to give. Their bodies shook with the force of their release until they collapsed in a heap upon the bed, spent and replete at last. Ragged breaths tore from their lungs as they sought for calm.

Nikolai gathered her close in his arms, spoon fashion, palming one of her swollen breasts tenderly. He pressed a kiss to her temple and cradled her hips with his, spearing his half swollen member, damp still from being inside her wetness, through her legs to rest in the pouting cleft of her sex.

"We will rest now, Julia mine."

"Yes," she breathed in agreement and settled back against him, sighing contentedly.

Before sleep claimed her in dark, tranquil waves, she heard her lover whisper into the night. "I can feel the moon. It is too soon...*too soon*, heaven help me."

She hadn't a clue what he was talking about—nor could she bring herself to wonder—she was far too spent and weary. It had been a long day...and an even longer night. Moments later she was asleep, safe in the protective circle of his arms, and his words were forgotten in the deep recesses of her mind.

And for the first time in too many long years, she knew that she wasn't alone.

* * * * *

Julia awoke in the bright light of the mid morning sun to hear the terrible cacophony of a wild howl coming from her bathroom. She jumped out of bed, wincing at the tender soreness between her legs, and raced to see what the horrible racket could be. She didn't know what to expect, but a gloriously nude and wet Nikolai standing in her shower stall was the last thing on her mind. Suddenly the events of the previous night came slamming through her mind, stealing her breath away with a rush of remembered passion.

He caught sight of her and cried, "This water is freezing! How do I work the hot spray?"

He sounded so pitiful, so wounded, that Julia couldn't help but laugh. "I thought you didn't have any electricity in your house, Nikolai. Shouldn't you be used to cold showers by now?"

"I have hot water. I draw it from a naturally heated spring near my house. I am not without creature comforts, I will have you know." He sounded positively indignant over the thought, and Julia fell into a peal of laughter once more. "Hot water, woman, and hurry before my appendages freeze off!"

"Well you'll have to do without because there isn't any hot water left," she informed him with devilish glee, loving to tease and torment him. "The other tenants have used it up by now. Everyone in the building shares the same hot water heater. It's late in the morning so you'll have to wait at least a couple of hours before there's enough warm water for a quick shower. Sorry."

Nikolai grimaced and soaped his hair and chest with a shocking swiftness. Julia knew she should leave him to his privacy, at least look away, but found that she couldn't even move. She was riveted by the froth of the soap bubbles over the firm muscles of his shoulders and chest. Mesmerized by the flow of water that ran in glistening torrents down the flat planes of his stomach, into the golden nest of hair that cushioned his impressively long, and not surprisingly flaccid penis. His testicles were heavy between his thighs, round and full as they swung with his hurried movements, despite the freezing spray. A flood of liquid desire swept through her, making her heart race, her breath pant and her knees weaken and tremble.

Nikolai abruptly paused in his movements, closed his eyes and inhaled deeply.

"I can smell your desire, love." He shuddered and his muscles contorted with alarming violence, making her gasp. His cock grew to immediate, shocking rigidity. "You should go, Julia. You are not ready for more of me just yet. I have to...calm down first. You need gentleness. Not rough play." His words were clipped, bitten out between his clenching teeth. His mouth looked swollen around his teeth, as if the words wanted to push their way out, but he would hold them back regardless.

That quickly Julia's mood changed, and her body flooded with a chill foreboding. He could *smell* her desire? As he had smelled her blood the night before when he'd taken her virginity? A thrill of something resembling fear swept through her. Instinctively she knew that not everything was right with Nikolai. What that was, she had no idea, but it was blatantly apparent in that moment as he stood shuddering beneath the spray of the water. His cock was impressive—massive—and Julia was shocked that he'd ever been able to fit inside of her at all. He was menacing in his stance and demeanor and his sudden arousal only added to that effect. Self preservation warned her to run, run as far away as her trembling legs could possibly carry her. But her heart ached with the knowledge that her lover suffered from some...*thing,* strange and unknown as it may be to her at the moment. Her heart bade her to stay, to ease the torment that was so plainly etched on every plane and feature of Nikolai's naked body.

Julia took a tentative step forward, heart pounding in her breast. Then another, slowly approaching the shower. She reached out her hand to touch, wanting only to soothe Nikolai's rigid, trembling muscles.

His hand shot out and captured her wrist in a nearly painful grip. When his eyes opened they blazed with a preternatural and menacing fire, glowing like two blue stars beneath his dripping wet hair. "Julia..." His voice was a low growl that made the hairs on the back of her nape stand up on end. "You. Have. To. Go. *Now*!" He threw her hand away as if it burned and crouched back into the shower, panting and shaking.

Julia cried out, in fear and worry—worry for him as well as for herself—and though she wanted to stay, to find out the reason why Nikolai was suddenly so *feral,* his iron command echoed in her mind and compelled her to turn and run from the room as if the very hounds of hell were snarling at her heels. When she reached the safe haven of her bedroom she heard Nikolai cry out—*howl*—and pound on the wall of the shower stall in some kind of fit. Her hands shook and her belly cramped, with fear or apprehension or yes, even desire, she wasn't certain. But something *was* obvious to her now.

Nikolai wasn't like other men. He was dangerous. He was unstable.

And God help her, she wanted him despite it all. Perhaps she even wanted him *because* of it all. His passionate extremes thrilled her to her core as nothing else ever had before, making her weak and breathless, passionate and eager, for anything and everything concerning him. His volatile emotions called to hers on an elemental level, exciting her to similar extremes, which both shocked and intrigued her. She didn't understand him or her reaction to him but regardless of that, she meant to find out as much about him as she could. She had to. Her heart demanded it. And Julia had never been able to deny her heart.

* * * * *

It was half an hour before Julia heard Nikolai turn off the water in the bathroom. She was sitting on her bed, garbed in a worn bathrobe, thinking on all the long moments she'd spent in Nikolai's company. Their first meeting when he'd licked her cheek, of all things. Their first date when he'd eaten so much with such heady appetite. The fact that he'd eaten mostly rare meats didn't escape her, in fact it alarmed her for reasons she couldn't rationally define as yet. She remembered how their first date had ended—how he'd enticed her to stay with wondrous kisses and caresses, then snarled at her without warning, to go, to run from him. And his movements were so alien. So unlike those of anyone she'd ever seen outside of a ballet. He moved gracefully, fluidly, using his body like a tool—a shell—to perform whatever function he so desired. He seemed separate from his own body somehow, even though he was quite obviously comfortable with it. She couldn't quite pin point why that bothered her, but it did. It really did.

His reflexes and senses were honed to a finite edge. He could smell things she could not. He could see well in the dark.

Goodness! If she didn't know better, she'd think he was an alien or something. Julia laughed at her own foolishness. It was obvious that Nikolai was different, but there was a limit to how different he could be. He was probably high strung, possibly medicated for temperamental difficulties like mania or even a panic disorder. His other peculiarities, well they could be explained. He was a wilderness man—he'd told her so himself—he lived in a place where finely developed motor skills and senses were essential, surely. He hunted for his own meat on a regular basis in order to survive, and that alone could account for why he was so seemingly different. He had a predatory air about him, there was no mistaking that. Perhaps she was overreacting just a little.

Then again…perhaps not.

Nikolai walked into the room then, still naked and dripping, and she let her thoughts rest for future contemplation. She watched him warily, never taking her eyes off of him. He looked normal. Gorgeous, sexy and lip smacking delicious, but still normal. But he looked larger today than he had the day before…and the day before. Though surely that was because he was unclothed. Clothing often disguised much about a person's size and physique.

"I could not find any towels." His voice was husky and strained, as if he'd used it too much.

"Oh. I'm sorry." Julia rose, careful to keep the bed between them. "I'll go find you one, just give me a minute."

"Do not worry about it, my Julia." He gave her a slight smile, obviously aware of her hesitancy around him. Then he shook his body, shuddering first from head then to shoulders then to midriff and down, sending water droplets flying about the room.

Julia yelped then giggled. He looked so adorable she couldn't help herself. It didn't bother her that he was getting water all over her carpet—it would dry. And this way she didn't have to give him one of her worn towels to use. That would have been too embarrassing for her to deal with just then. With one last shudder Nikolai stilled. His hair was no longer dripping and his body was surprisingly dry.

"Well, that's one way of doing it, I guess. You probably don't spend much time washing towels," Julia teased him.

Nikolai gave her a toothy grin, eyes shining, and began gathering his discarded clothing from about the room.

"What's wrong, Nikolai?" She hadn't known that she meant to speak the words until they were already out of her mouth and echoing in the air between them.

"What do you mean? Nothing is wrong. Everything is good." He clearly averted his eyes from hers when he spoke, and his accent was thick—a clear sign that he *was* disturbed.

"You know what I mean." She was surprised that her voice could be so firm when inside she was shaking like a leaf. "I can tell that something's bothering you. If you would just tell me what it is, instead of barking at me when the mood strikes, maybe I could help you sort it out."

Nikolai was silent for a very long moment and Julia was sure that he wasn't going to respond, which made her more than a little testy. But then he sank down heavily on the bed, and hung his head down low in another of his strange, graceful movements. His eyes rose up to meet hers, blazing out from beneath hanks of hair that fell over his brow.

"I have been barking at you and I am sorry, Julia mine. You do not deserve that kind of treatment, it is unforgivable of me."

"Oh, good grief, everybody gets a little pissy now and then. It's not an unforgivable sin by any means. But if you'd just tell me what's bothering you, maybe I could understand where you're coming from a little bit better and help to calm you down some." She ignored the feelings of caution inside of her and went to sit next to him, rubbing his back with comforting strokes.

"Julia..." His voice cracked. "I do not think you can help me with this." He shuddered under her hand.

"Try me," she urged.

Nikolai's knuckles popped as he clenched his hands on his thighs. Julia tried to keep her eyes from straying inevitably upwards, but failed. His cock was semi-erect, even after his long shower in freezing water. Then something else drew her attention. The muscles of his abdomen rolled like ripples in a pond, alarmingly and with much ferocity. It was one of the strangest things Julia had ever seen and definitely not normal.

"Are you sick?" she asked, desperately worried about him.

"I am..."

"You are? Well, no matter what is wrong with you, we can get you well again." She pulled him close, wanting—*needing*—to give comfort.

"I am not sick." He took a deep, shuddering breath before he spoke again. "Julia, I want you to know that what is between us...I do not take it lightly. I have strong feelings for you. I know it sounds...well I know that sometimes men say things to women that they do not mean. But I mean it, I really do. I feel like I have known you far longer than I have. I felt it the first moment I saw you. I do not want to destroy what is between us by burdening you with my…I do not want to burden you."

Julia had never heard him sound so hesitant. So earnest but so desperately alone. If he really felt that way, then his odd behavior was even more of an enigma. And though she'd only known him for three days, she realized that she too felt a bond with him. She had from the first. Why else would she have given herself to him, after she'd waited and remained a virgin for so long a time? Yes, he was attractive. Yes, he was interesting and thrilling to be around. And while she'd always dreamed of being sought out by just that type of man, she admitted to herself that it wasn't really enough to get her *involved* with one. And she was definitely involved with Nikolai, as unexpected and strange as that fact may be, it was still a fact. One she couldn't deny to herself or to him.

Her next words were from her heart and she gave no thought to holding them back, no matter that they made her vulnerable. "I feel the same way about you Nikolai. I don't know why, but I do. I would have never gone back out with you after our first date if that weren't so. You scared me that first night, when you rushed me from your suite, but you also made me feel more alive than ever I had before. Just being out on your balcony with you—dining with you—was one of the most wonderful and magical experiences of my life. There's something about you. It calls to me, deep inside. And that's why I want to help you now, Nikolai. I can see that something is wrong, something I don't understand. Please, let me help you. Tell me what's making you act so strange. Together we can work it out, I'm sure of that."

Nikolai's massive frame shuddered once again, with enough force to make her own body quake along with it. "You will run from me. You will not want to have anything more to do with me if I tell you."

"You don't know that for sure. Trust me, maybe I'll surprise you," she said coaxingly, trying to lighten the heavy oppressive feelings that were assailing her.

Nikolai's hair, which seemed oddly longer today than it had the night before, tickled her shoulder as he turned to lean his forehead against hers. He reached up and stroked her cheek with a tender caress and breathed down into her mouth four gently spoken words.

"I am a wolf."

Chapter Nine

ꟗ

The hairs stood up all over her body, signaling an instinctive alarm at his words, but her voice was steady when she asked, "A wolf?"

"I am a wolf. I am not a human."

"Forgive me for being obtuse, but you look pretty human to me Nikolai." She pulled away from him with a frown.

"I am a...werewolf." He twisted the word out of his mouth as if he weren't accustomed to it. "An alpha *Bodark* or *Wawkalak*—both are names in my country for werewolves or shape shifters. I am the leader of my pack, the first in command, the strongest and most feared of my kind. And I am...changing. It is too soon in the month—which alarms me more than I can explain to you—but nevertheless I cannot deny that I *am* changing. "

"You're serious."

"I have never been more serious." He reached for her but she pulled back before she even thought about how that would make him feel. He gritted his teeth and let his hands drop back down onto his thighs. "I wanted to wait to tell you, let you grow more accustomed to me before I revealed what I am. But something is not right. I have never been so out of control. And I am afraid I might have put you in danger by staying near you...yet I cannot leave. I need you too much to run from you, even if it is to keep you safe. And I am torn in two because of it."

Julia didn't know what to say. Thinking back on all that she knew about it she found his claim believable...and yet such a thing was impossible, surely. She didn't believe in the supernatural. She never had.

"If you are...what you say you are, then prove it. Show me something. Do something that only a werewolf could do—change into a wolf if you want—prove to me that you're not yanking my chain."

Nikolai cocked his head to the side. "Yanking your chain?"

"You know what I mean—your English isn't so bad," she fired out in exasperation. "Prove to me that you're not joking or lying."

"I cannot simply change fully into a wolf on command, not at will. I am at the mercy of the pull of the moon. Only when it is full can I assume my lupine form."

"Well show me something, anything. Make me believe you, because if you don't I swear I'm going to boot you out of my apartment so fast your head will spin."

"Very well. I will prove it." He rose from the bed and walked to the far side of the room. He turned and faced her from beneath a wild tangle of hair. "Do not be afraid. I will not hurt you, I promise."

With that he threw back his head, bared his elongated incisors and let loose a mighty roar. The room vibrated with the sound and seemed to close in on them, causing Julia's heart to stop for an alarming moment.

Julia screamed in fright. The tattered remnants of her dream, in which Nikolai had bitten her neck in a fit of passion, came back to haunt her then and she became even more afraid. She scrambled back across the bed, fell to the floor, rose on shaking legs and darted for the bedroom door in a panic. Nikolai reached it before she did, even though he'd been much further away.

"Do you believe me now?"

"G-get out of my way," she cried.

"Why? Do you fear me now? Have I disgusted you?" His eyes grew dark and menacing.

"How can you be…w-what you say you are? *You're really not human*?" Her last words died to a frantic whisper as her well-known and comfortable world turned upside down. Suddenly everything she'd believed in all of her life seemed a lie. There *were* mythical creatures out there in the world, unexplainable and magical things. And one of them was standing right in front of her.

"I am a wolf. A wolf that loves you with all of his heart. You are my mate for life, Julia. As soon as I get whatever is wrong with me sorted out, I will show you how glorious this bond between us can be."

Julia was too startled, too frightened and unnerved to pay any real attention to what he was saying to her. She'd just had the surprise of her life and wasn't having any luck getting beyond that for the moment. Adrenaline surged unchecked through her system and she struck out before she thought, landing a forceful blow squarely between his legs with her fist. As he doubled over in pain and surprise Julia took the opportunity to shove him aside, jerk open the door, and race out of the room. Her first instinct was to run, far and fast, away from him, even as her heart cried out that what she was doing was unfair and against her growing affection for the man she'd just wounded. So she ran, stumbling over any obstacles in her path on her mad dash to the door of her apartment.

There was a forceful tug on the loose sash of her robe and she stumbled to the floor, crying out in surprise. She turned and saw Nikolai loom up over her menacingly.

"Do not run, you only make me want to chase you when you do and it excites me far too much," he gritted out between his sharp teeth before reaching down, grabbing her by her upper arms and raising her off of the floor. He held her up, feet dangling off of the floor a good twelve inches, and shook her slightly. "You hurt me, Julia, most grievously. But do you see how I do not hurt you in retaliation for that blow you dealt me? I would never willingly hurt you. If you believe nothing else, then please believe that." He shook her again.

Julia felt tears begin to flow unchecked down her cheeks. She was so torn. On the one hand she was terrified of Nikolai and on the other...her heart ached with the force of her emotions, emotions that she dare not even name or examine too closely just now. "N-N-Nikolai, I'm sorry." Her voice broke on a sob. "But I don't know what to think—what to do. I barely know you but...*God! I don't know what to say*. You scared me."

Nikolai gathered her close in his arms. Her feet still dangled a good foot off of the floor but she ceased her struggle with him, went limp in his embrace and allowed him to comfort her. It always felt so right—so perfect—to be in his arms, and this time was no exception. She needed him to hold her.

"I am sorry I scared you. I suppose I should have found a better way to prove my claim to you. But now do you believe me when I say that I am not like you?"

She choked out a laugh around her tears. "How could I not believe you? You've got *fangs* for goodness sake! My god! You're not human, not human, *not human*." She started to hyperventilate as the thought slammed home again and again in her dazed mind. Nikolai quickly carried her to her small couch, sat her down, and shoved her head down between her knees.

"I am sorry for your upset over this Julia. If I could have given you more time to grow accustomed to this truth I would have, believe me."

Julia rose, feeling lightheaded but more in control of herself again. "But how did this happen to you? Were you bitten by a werewolf—is that how it works?—like in the stories you hear or the movies on television?"

Nikolai laughed darkly in disgust. "Brianna has told me about your werewolf myths as I had never heard of such tales, living so far removed from human society. But rest assured that none of those horrific stories are grounded in true reality. We are far different. In fact I have never heard tales of any others like us."

"Brianna knows what you are? Wait a minute! D-did you say 'us'? There are more l-like you?" She shivered. Her body was a quagmire of discontent, so many questions raced through her mind, each more alarming and confusing than the last. She'd had too much of a shock to think clearly, to react rationally about anything for the moment.

"There are many more like me. My whole village is comprised of others like myself. But let me assure you, before you ask, that we are not at all as your myths portray us. We do not feast on human flesh, hearts, or tongues. I have heard about those terrible lies and they disgust me. We are a proud race—a separate race entirely from humans, evolved from similar ancestors I have no doubt, but separate now in all the ways that matter—and we keep to ourselves. In fact, we prefer a peaceful life, in the wilderness, far away from humans."

"You mean you've always been like this?"

"Yes." He smiled at her incredulous expression. "Though it is a little more complicated than what you are probably thinking. When I was born—when those of my kind are born—we do not automatically experience the change every month. Our cycles work a little differently until puberty."

"I can't believe this is really true. You're a werewolf. It sounds so crazy. So what happens when the moon is full in a couple of weeks? Do you get all furry and slobbery or…what?"

"Well my body is in an ever constant state of transformation. As the moon grows or shrinks so, too, do our lupine selves."

"What do you mean? Don't you know exactly what day you'll change?"

"No. I will likely change on the eve of the moon at its fullest." He took a deep breath and rolled his shoulders as if he were growing impatient with the conversation. "I am alpha—the strongest male of my pack, my family—and because of that I can hold off my change the longest. I can stay in my bipedal form the longest, and if I should chose, I can stay in my wolf form the longest as well. But basically our cycles work like this. When the moon is full we change into wolves—well not exactly wolves but something very close—so close you could not tell us apart from a full blood wolf unless you were an expert, except maybe for our size—we are quite large in lupine form."

He paused and shifted again. "As the moon wanes we change back into human-like creatures, but we are not entirely human. We are faster, stronger, and have keener senses than full blood humans. As the moon moves into its darkest phase, the new moon, we are less muscular and our fangs are not in evidence unless you look very closely. And then, as the moon waxes our bodies grow larger, our hair and incisors lengthen and we move with an even greater swiftness and power…until we change into wolves once more. When we are young we only grow surly or more 'furry' as you said, it is not until puberty that we change fully."

"You talk as if this is so…normal. I've just had the fright of my life. To think that such a thing is possible. It's out of this world," she marveled.

"It is normal to me. Soon you will grow to accept it and it will be normal to you as well."

"I don't think so. I can't ever see myself ever getting used to the idea. Just think, if werewolves exist then what about vampires and ghosts and trolls and elves? What other mythological beings are out there, just keeping to themselves as you have?" Another thought occurred to her then. "Why are you here, exactly? What could possibly make you want to leave your home and be here amongst so many humans? Aren't you afraid of being discovered?"

"I did not lie to you when you asked me before why I was here. Brianna, my cousin's wife, is pregnant and close to term with our first known interspecies offspring. Her company—The Living Forest Enterprises—needed to conduct some legal business with her but she couldn't risk the chance of an early birth during a trip over here. She and the child she carries had a much greater chance of being discovered than I. So I came in her stead as her emissary to the company, and took care of things for her here."

Julia saw a flash of his fangs as he spoke and started to hyperventilate again. Nikolai's concern for her was etched plainly on his features but she couldn't calm down long enough to appreciate or remark on it. The thought that she was sitting next to something—someone—not human, tormented her. And she'd lain with him—had sex with him—for god's sake. Though the memory frightened and alarmed her, it also incredibly aroused her and that realization caused her breathing to become even more erratic.

"Calm down, love, I can smell your fear and it is tearing my heart to pieces to know that I have caused this response in you. You have no need to be so afraid of me. I would never willingly hurt you."

Julia refused to dwell on the fact that his glowing eyes averted when he spoke those last words, or that his voice was unsteady as he trembled once again. Her breath sobbed in harsh, desperate bellows as she fought valiantly to calm.

"Then w-why did you push me aw-way those times? Why did you g-grow so angry with m-me?"

"I was not angry with you, only with myself for losing control. I said I would never willingly hurt you and I meant that, with all of my being I meant that. But, since meeting you," he shook so forcefully that the couch shifted with his movements, "I have not been myself. I have come close to losing control of my emotions and instincts, and though I have never harmed an innocent while in my wolf's state, I fear that I might accidentally hurt you. My emotions are in turmoil when you are near me and I have never had to deal with such a loss of control. I do not know what I am capable of when I lose myself like this."

"But I thought you only changed when the moon was full," she whispered fearfully.

"We do and it is a while yet before the moon will be full this month. But I am changing despite that. Despite the moon's phase. And that is the most frightening thing of all," he whispered back.

Chapter Ten

ꟗ

Julia bit her lip to keep from keening aloud her alarm upon seeing the new and dangerous glow that emanated out from Nikolai's eyes with his words. It was obvious that he was having trouble keeping himself subdued around her. He looked restless enough to climb the walls at the very least. His muscles roiled and shifted and her eyes were immediately drawn down over his glorious nudity. How fear and desire could mix so exquisitely within her she would never understand, but these were exactly the emotions she felt at the sight of so much bare, golden skin. Then Nikolai's shoulders shifted and popped in their sockets and worry came to the fore. Worry for Nikolai…and for her.

She gritted her teeth with enough force to hear them grind together in her head. Now was the time for an inner reckoning. Was she going to tell Nikolai to leave and try to forget the events of the past couple of hours? Was there still time to do such a thing without bringing injury to her heart and her sanity? Was that even what she wanted to do?

No, emphatically no.

She'd always taken the easy route through her relationships with people, preferring to keep everything simple and uncomplicated, never risking her heart or her emotions. Well now she'd taken a chance, a big one, and bedded a man knowing full well that for her sex would mean more than just a one night stand with a relative stranger. And that man, her lover, was in need of her now, it was plain to see. Was she hesitant about his animalistic tendencies? Yes. But did they turn her off, did she want him less because of them? No, definitely not. In fact she was more intrigued, on many levels—not only sexually—by his claims of being a werewolf.

Though this situation was far from a normal one in the scheme of love and relationships between people, Julia felt a need—a compulsion—to follow it through as though it were one. She couldn't push Nikolai away from her simply because he was different. Nor could she believe that he would let things get so bad in himself that he harmed her. She was sure he would leave her before such a thing happened. She trusted him, no matter that she barely knew it. She felt, deep within her heart and soul, that this man was well worth any risk she might take.

"What will we do?" she asked, stressing "we".

Nikolai looked at her long and hard, as if searching for some hesitancy or weakness in her sudden resolve. When he found none he shuddered and turned to draw her closer, careful to move slowly lest he frighten her off. "I do not know, Julia. Perhaps this weakness of mine will pass. Perhaps it is merely from my being caged up in the walls of this city. I do not know. I only know that your nearness both soothes and exacerbates my condition."

"Is there anything we can do to take your mind off of it for a while? Maybe there is something that can help," she suggested, settling against him, ignoring an instinctive nervous thrill at being so close to him now.

Immediately Nikolai's cock lengthened and hardened, engorging with a sudden rush of blood. Julia couldn't have failed to notice it had she tried. The great plumed head on his shaft bobbed against the arm she had settled around his waist, demanding her attention with a mind of its own. Her body responded instantly, causing her nipples to swell and become erect under her robe and her cunt to tingle and grow wet with her arousal. She shifted in her seat, to ease the sudden, empty ache between her legs, but Nikolai stilled her movements easily.

He reached over and pulled her across his lap, settling her thighs on either side of his so that she straddled him. "Kissing might help," he said in a coaxing murmur.

"Only kissing?" she asked and pressed a soft kiss to his jaw. She couldn't believe that she was so open to this sexuality between them, but it felt so completely right to give in to it that she never even considered slowing things down.

"Maybe touching too..." He shuddered beneath her as her hands began roving over the planes of his chest with a will all their own.

"Anything else?" she teased.

"Grrrrrr..." Somehow this new guttural cry of his only served to heighten her arousal. It did not frighten her in the least. "Maybe...*trakhat'sya*—fucking...would help."

His coarse language made her clit pulse with anticipation. "Maybe it would at that," she agreed.

Julia leaned down and kissed his lips, marveling at their silken texture, their decadent masculine flavor. Nikolai kept his hands at her thighs, as if worried that if he were to grab her and take control of the kiss she would bolt. And perhaps she would have, at that; Julia wasn't sure what would have happened. But just by holding himself in check, he reaffirmed the thought in her mind that he would not harm her. She felt safer because of it and grew bold in her exploration of his body.

His cock pressed against the apex of the thighs and in the position she was now, her vagina was spread wide so that her wet flesh rubbed lightly against him. She shifted, moving her hips closer against him, and sighed in pleasure when his shaft slid against the swollen button of her clit. Her hands kneaded into the heavy muscles of his upper arms, testing his strength like a curious kitten. In the meanwhile, Nikolai's hands slid against the plumpness of her thighs and knees as they gripped his sides. His hands, splayed wide, encompassed most of that area, and made her feel unexpectedly small beneath them.

Julia let her mouth slide off of his, reveling in the harsh booming breaths he took—clear evidence of her effect on his senses—and trailed open mouthed kisses down his chin and throat. She scooted back, pressed her mouth into the rise of muscle on his chest and scraped her fingernails lightly over his nipples, making them grow as hard as hers were already.

Nikolai groaned and shifted slightly beneath her, once again drawing her attention to his marble-hard penis as it brushed against the bottom of one of her breasts. She moved her kisses lower and licked the hard kernel of his nipple. Nikolai's hands stilled against her and she stroked the rippling planes of his stomach, teasingly, coaxingly, seeing how far up she could drive him before he took command of the situation. When he didn't move but for the unsteady rise and fall of his chest, she rewarded him by wrapping her hands around his cock and pumping him once, twice, three loving times. She was surprised to note that he was uncircumcised, with a plump yet delicate foreskin that moved beneath her hands as she squeezed and thrust.

He nearly bucked her off of him, so violently did he rise up beneath her. He groaned ragged and loud, and she smiled against his nipple. She blew across his saliva-moistened flesh and was pleased to hear him groan once again. All her hesitancy and worry fled as if it never had been and she lost herself to the thrill of being with him. He smelled heavenly, with just a hint of her soap mingled in with the woodsy musk of his usual fragrance, and she breathed him in deeply, savoring his essence. She scraped her teeth gently across him, making him gasp, and then she scooted off of him like a monkey and rested on her knees before him on the floor.

"I've never done this before. Tell me if I do anything wrong," she breathed coquettishly.

Before he could reply Julia spread his knees with her hands, leaned in and pressed her lips to the head of his cock.

"Ah, *der'mo*! Shit, yes, *aahhhh*," he groaned, spearing his fingers into the thickness of the hair on her head, tangling them there.

If he responds that way to just a kiss, she thought, *how will he respond to something a little more*?

She found out when she let the crown of him into the ring of her lips and flicked him lightly with her tongue. He thrust up against her and pulled her head down at the same time, spearing himself deep into her mouth until he nudged the back of her throat.

"Oh, Julia, did I hurt you?" he asked in a worried rush.

He had surprised her, yes, but he hadn't hurt her. In fact, she was curious to see how far she could take him in her mouth and throat. He was so large she knew she couldn't take all of him without gagging, but she could try and see just how much she could handle of his delicious sugar dick. She deliberately relaxed the muscles in her throat and slowly sank her mouth down on him, her movements answer enough—she hoped—to his question. When it felt like she was swallowing the head of him she sucked, careful of her teeth on him, and moved back.

"That feels so…so very good." He moaned in wonder, sounding pleasantly surprised, as if he'd never been inside of a woman's mouth.

She hummed against him, in agreement with his words. It did feel good to have him at her mercy this way, in thrall to the things she was doing to him. He tasted delicious, like nothing she'd ever imagined, both wondrously and mysteriously male at the same time. She palmed his heavy testicles, lifting and gently squeezing them in her hands, eager to explore the complex weapon between his legs and discover what pleased him best.

Sinking her mouth back down on him, she realized that her body was equally as affected by this love play as her mind was. A thin trail of wetness leaked down from her pussy onto her leg. She moved one hand from his sac and felt the wetness of her quim with her middle finger. It felt so good to be touched there, no matter that it was with her own hand, and she couldn't resist rubbing her clit in time with the bobbing movements of her head on his penis. She grew bolder and sank her face even farther down on him, ignoring the slight discomfort in her throat as she took him deep.

The smacking, slurping noises her mouth made as she went down on him turned her on even more, until her nipples and clit were swelled and begging for friction—any kind of friction—to ease their tingling ache. She deliberately shifted so that her nipples rubbed against the dusting of crisp hair on his legs and increased the tempo of her fingers on her clit accordingly. The satiny texture of his cock slid in and out of her mouth, filling her senses with the taste, feel and scent of him. His balls butted against her chin as he bucked once more into her throat.

"Julia—*aaaah, my sweet Julia*—slow down. I'm going to...I'm going to..." He growled and bucked reflexively when she paid his broken command no heed and, in fact, moved her mouth on him even more rapidly.

Julia moaned against him as he thrust deep into her mouth, vibrating the length of him even as she thrust and withdrew over him, and then licked the rim of his foreskin as it was pushed up over the tip of his cock with the pumping motions of her hand. He was lush and thick, tasting both sweet and salty at the same time, and she moaned again in her pleasure over all the unique discoveries she was making.

The flesh of his cock trembled with a tiny, swift heartbeat. Nikolai went rigid beneath her then thrust up with a force that unseated her mouth from him. He roared and the thick, creamy jettison of his release splashed on her neck and throat.

His hands were fists in her hair, but the tingling pain at her scalp only made her grin triumphantly, because it was proof that she had succeeded in making him lose himself in the moment. She, a previously untried virgin, had tamed the beast in him if but for a short while.

Still curious, seeking to explore everything there was to know about her lover's body, she reached out and ran her fingers through the pool of semen that dripped down her flesh. It was hot, viscous and wet in texture, and smelled of sweet woodland rain. Darting her tongue out she dared to taste of it and found the flavor much to her liking, a combination of sweet, spicy and tart all at the same time. Wanting more of the delicious fruits of her labors she bent and sucked the last pearling droplets of come from the opening of Nikolai's throbbing cock.

"*Mmmmm*, delicious," she purred, smacking her lips.

"*Ebat'-kopat'*! Woman, the things you do to me!" He let out a bark of a laugh then smoothed her hair back with less than steady fingers. "You are not hurt? I was rough, I know. I am sorry—"

"Don't apologize." She quickly laid her sperm moistened hands against his mouth before she even thought how distasteful he might find that and was therefore surprised when he licked the small traces of his release away from her fingertips. "I loved every moment of it," she finished raggedly, heart racing at the evidence of his earthy and shameless appetites.

"So did I, Julia mine. And now…" he paused dramatically, leaning down to sweep her into his arms, "it is my turn to have you at my mercy." He rose from his position on the couch and carried her to her bedroom.

Nikolai laid her down upon the coverlet then immediately covered her with his body. The sun was high in the sky by now, creating a bright golden halo about his head as he came down upon her. He rubbed her sensuously with the whole length of his frame, from head to toe, writhing against her with the exotic and otherworldly contortions of his heavily muscled form. Her breathing hitched as she saw a flash of his fangs, but he soothed her with a gentle press of his lips to hers, kissing her with a sweetness that brought tears of remorse for feeling that instant of fear.

With desperate hands she clutched him to her, parting her lips and inviting his tongue inside for a deeper exploration. Giving her time to pull away should she choose to do so, he inched his tongue into her mouth. When she only opened her mouth wider and licked along his tongue with her own, he relaxed a little, and let his enthusiasm show once again. He caressed the roof of her mouth, her teeth and lips, thrusting and withdrawing, skillful and expert in every erotic motion he made. He stole her breath and gave her back his own until she was moaning and writhing beneath him. His kiss alone brought her to the edge of pleasure, driving her completely mindless and wild as it went on and on and on.

Julia shrieked into his mouth and pulled at his hair, anxious for more of him. He obliged her needs, spreading wide her thighs and pulling her up to him so that she straddled him as he leaned back on his knees in the bed. Slowly he set her down upon his rock-hard cock, until she was fighting him to impale herself with the roughness she was craving. He tried to hold her back, to pace their movements, but ultimately she won out because—in truth—he wanted that roughness too. With a violent motion he pulled her down as he rose up to meet her, impaling her to the hilt with one, slick thrust.

There was a scream and, too late, Julia realized that it had broken free from her own lips. Two tears squeezed out of the corners of her eyes, tears of exquisite pleasure—not pain—and Nikolai licked them away with a tiny murmur of feral appreciation. He trembled savagely in her embrace, pulling her out of the exquisite daze she'd been languishing in as she felt a thrill of worry race through her.

"Are you okay?" she asked breathlessly.

He shook against her once more and whimpered like a wounded pup. "Som…something is…*argh*!" He jerked against her, thrusting deep into her, shocking a pleasure-filled moan right out of her. "Something is not…not right." He began to mutter thickly in a long stream of Russian, clearly becoming agitated. His hips pistoned in and out of her in lightning quick strokes, bringing her quickly to the precipice of her climax. "Forgive me, forgive me," he repeated over and over, even as he pumped himself into her.

There was nothing to forgive. Julia was having the ride of her life and enjoying every wondrous moment of it. Nikolai quaked again and again—even his cock vibrated inside of her with his unsteady movements—before he threw her down onto the mattress beneath him and pounded into her with unrestrained savagery. His mouth burrowed into the flesh of her neck until she felt the scrape of his incisors…and then she was soaring.

She cried, she wailed, she shrieked and moaned. Her entire body was swamped with exquisite pleasure. Every second that passed by thrust her up higher and higher into her release, until she felt full of starlight, full of moonlight, full to bursting with *him*. In the back of her mind she heard Nikolai's howl of satisfaction as he bowed his body against her, head held back as he brayed, and pumped his come into her welcoming body. Even though he had already found one release, he filled her to overflowing with his seed until it coated her sex like thick, rich, silky cream. It was wondrous, heavenly and perfect in every way but one; Nikolai immediately pulled away from her, howling and snarling, drawing her out of her release as swiftly as if he'd dashed cold water onto her.

"Nikolai! What's wrong?" she asked in a panic. His muscles bulged and rippled alarmingly. His bones popped with audible volume and she cried out, "Omigod! You need a doctor—or *something*—you're going spastic."

"No doctors." His voice was nearly unrecognizable, bestial. "Please...*argh, pleeeease*," he howled.

"Okay, no doctors," she hurried to reassure him.

"No. Plea...ompf." He bowed off of the bed before he could finish. Several seconds crawled by as Julia went down beside him, sobbing, and tried to help him back up. "Please, you must," he groaned again, contorting in her arms. "You must tie me up."

"What? Are you nuts? I can't do that," she exclaimed. "You need help, not torture."

"Listen to me! I am not myself. You are in danger." Each sentence was clipped and rushed, so that she barely understood him. "Tie me up. Restrain me until I am calm again."

Julia jumped back as he threw back his head and roared, a sound that chilled her to her very bones. His face shifted and blurred before her very eyes, until Julia feared she would faint with her mixture of emotions—remembered pleasure that still coursed through her veins even now—along with her fear, worry, and panic over Nikolai's distress.

"Do it, woman!" he barked out. "Tie me to the bed. Tight. So that I cannot break free. *Please*."

Julia jumped up and ran to the coat closet that was just behind the front door to her home as fast as her quaking legs could carry her. For what seemed like endless moments she rummaged through some old moving boxes, left over from when she'd first moved into the apartment, until, finally she found a ball of nylon rope. "Goodness I hope there's enough, he's a big guy," she muttered to herself.

She raced back to her bedroom and caught sight of Nikolai as he tried to crawl his way up her bed, even as his body was wracked by alarming shudders and contortions, each more violent than the last. "Let me help you," she managed to say around the tears that choked her throat.

He was even heavier than he looked, which was surprising, and it took quite a lot of effort between the two of them to get him into the bed. He sprawled onto his back and yelped as though in pain, which wouldn't have surprised Julia in the least, considering the way his muscles and bones were straining. "Hurry," he panted out, moving his hands and feet so that they were close to the four posts of her bed frame.

Growing up in the country sometimes had its advantages, as it did in this instance when Julia began knotting his wrists to the bed. She tied expert and immovable knots around him, recalling all the times she'd secured her horses or cattle on the farm. Unfortunately the rope was only long enough to tie off both of his wrists. There wasn't nearly enough length left over to reach his ankles. Nikolai thrashed in the bed, nearly unseating himself before he calmed again unexpectedly. "Julia, you have to tie my feet. There's no telling what I will do to escape if this gets any worse. I don't want to be given the slightest advantage."

"But I don't have any more rope! I'm surprised I found that much," she cried.

"You must think of something…please…*please*!" He choked out the last and Julia realized how much his pride must have been suffering at this indignity in front of her.

Julia wracked her brain and then an idea struck. She tripped in her haste to reach her dresser and threw open the top drawer. It was short work to plunge her hands into its recesses and uncover her only pair of silk stockings—a luxury so precious that she hadn't even worn it to the soiree the night before, preferring to save them for the most special of occasions—and carry them with her as she turned and flew into the bathroom. There she found a pair of scissors and, wincing her regret at the loss, sliced them neatly in half. Not wasting any time she made her way back to Nikolai and brandished her treasure.

"God, I hope these work," she muttered breathlessly before setting to work on his ankles.

Moments later he was secure, ankles and wrists tied neatly and efficiently to their posts. And it was none too soon, because the tremors that wracked Nikolai increased in frequency and intensity. He growled and snarled, roared and howled, struggling with startling violence against his bonds. Julia feared that the neighbors would hear and alert the police, but minutes passed…then half an hour…an entire hour passed and there were no angry visitors pounding on her door demanding to know who was being murdered. Nikolai's struggles caused the bed to groan beneath him time and time again, but the bonds held and he could not free himself no matter how hard he tried. And he tried very, very hard.

The sun sank low in the sky, casting eerie shadows about the room, but Julia never left his side, even when he screamed at her to go, to run. She knew that her leaving would only place him in even greater danger—what if he had a heart attack, or an aneurysm from the trauma of all of his struggles?—and she understood, too, that deep down he really wanted her to stay. In his too brief flashes of calm sanity he even thanked her for staying, for giving him water when his mouth grew parched and bathing the sweat from his body as it poured off of him in rivulets. Her nearness was a comfort to him, even as it was a torture. Julia wasn't about to abandon him, she just couldn't.

He needed her. And no one had ever really needed her before—not like this—emotionally, physically and mentally. Even as she hated the circumstances behind the unique experience, she found she liked it a little bit too. It was nice to know that she could bring comfort to him, no matter how great or small. It felt good to care for him. And as that thought came so too did another and another and another, tumbling into her brain with the wildness of a storm until she realized something that made her head spin out of control and her heart to quail in her breast.

Good heavens! She was falling in love with the beast.

Chapter Eleven

꧁

Long hours passed and with them came the dawn and the moment of decisions for Julia. She wasn't scheduled to go into work until later that night, but she was scheduled for her once weekly painting class, which lasted all day. Unfortunately, if she missed more than three days in the course she would fail, and it was more than difficult for her to shirk her duty and ditch a day of school. But her indecision over the choice that circumstance had presented to her lasted no more than a minute. Nikolai needed her to be with him until he could safely be unrestrained and he was far more important than any class, no matter how difficult or costly it would be for her to miss. In truth, any human being would have been worth it to her, but that was especially true of him. He was growing more and more dear to her with each passing hour.

She was learning more and more about him and with each new thing she learned, she came that much closer to loving him. Truly and deeply loving him.

Nikolai, in his now nearly delirious state, talked on and on—strings of nonsensical words mostly—aloud to her. Much of the time his words were in swift Russian, beautifully articulated sounds that pulled at her heartstrings in the most endearing of ways. But sometimes he spoke in English, heavily accented at times, and then clipped and imperiously proper, as though he were British, at others. And though much of what he said was feverish ramblings, some of what he said served to uncover bits and pieces of his nature to her. Regardless, she listened closely to everything that he said, not wanting to miss a single word he spoke. Simply enjoying the sound of his melodious voice.

He was absolutely fascinating to her, because of both who and what he was.

At one point during the long night, he had spoken—as if to a child—to someone in his memories and luckily the words had been in English so that Julia could understand him. Julia deducted, after hours of scattered tidbits tossed out from Nikolai's parched lips, that the other participant in the conversation was his younger brother, Dragel. He was admonishing him thoroughly for getting himself and their other brother Jarus, in trouble with hunters. Nikolai had saved them from certain death, or at least it sounded that way to Julia, at great risk to himself and the pack.

His brothers had gone through their first change without waiting for the pack to guide them on the hunt and had struck off on their own through the wilderness. They had come across poachers and been hunted like vermin, for their pelts. Nikolai had saved them…exactly how she wasn't sure, beyond the fact that the hunters had died by Nikolai's hand. Wisely she hadn't wanted to know the details—they would have scared the life out of her, surely. It was obvious from his one sided conversation that he was trying to come up with a fitting punishment for his brothers' mischief.

It was an interesting story to be sure, though difficult to piece together with only Nikolai's one-sided ramblings. Julia hoped that he got well soon so that he could fill in the blanks of the story for her. Well, some of them anyway.

And, too, Nikolai spoke of the exhilaration of the change. Though Julia found his words hard to believe considering the obvious torture he was going through now because of it. She had been lead to understand that this particular instance was not the norm for him or his kind and had to remind herself of that, as worrisome as it was. He spoke of the freedom and the excitement of bounding over the snow and brush. How the smells assailed him like thousands of layers of paint, each one with a rich color all its own. Julia could almost scent the wild reindeer on the wind, the stag, and the hare, as he spoke of them. Delicious and wild they were as they ran from their natural predator, the wolf.

It was then that she realized they hadn't eaten all the day long, so she prepared them both a bowl of chicken noodle soup. She had to spoon the broth into Nikolai's mouth and he'd fought her like a wild man, but she'd managed to force some of the food into him, along with some cool water. Shortly after he had grown violent again, jerking at his bonds with an animalistic fury and roaring at her when she strayed to close, baring his long canines at her. His eyes were like torches in his face, burning at her in rage and desperation all at once.

"Where are the stars?" His voice drew her out of her memories just then and she scooted her rickety chair, which she'd dragged from the living room, closer to him. But not close enough that he could have grabbed her should he manage to break free of his restraints. She wasn't that foolish, no matter how deep in thrall with him she was becoming.

"There are no stars, Niki," she said. "It's morning already."

"I miss the moooooooon," he howled mournfully and it made her heart ache to hear his obvious suffering.

"You'll see the moon soon," she promised him, hoping it wasn't a lie she was telling him. He seemed so sick, she wondered if he would ever get well. There was nothing she could do to help him, so she prayed fervently that he would somehow heal on his own. "And the stars."

"Julia? Julia, my heart, you have come. At last you have come. I have waited so long for you."

"I've been here all night. I've never left."

"Brianna came to Ivan, but you never came to me. I waited and I called into the night for you but you never came."

His voice broke, full of anguished suffering. "You never came."

"*Shhh*, you're not well, Nikolai. But I promise you that I won't leave you like this," she swore fervently.

"Julia!" he roared.

"I'm here Nikolai, please calm down," she sobbed, aching to see him so tormented and fevered. She soothed a cool washcloth against his brow, jumping when he made a move to bite her.

Several moments passed and he seemed to calm once more. Then, "Julia?" he called to her softly, his voice hoarse from so many shouts and roars.

"Yes, Nikolai? I'm here. Can you hear me?"

"I am sorry that I have done this to you—put you in this frightful position. That I have worried you so."

"There's nothing to be sorry for, love." She sought to reassure him, though she wasn't certain he could hear or understand her words. "Just hurry up and get well for me, okay?"

"Will you kiss me, Julia? Now, when I can feel your lips on mine and hold on to the memory of it when I am...not myself."

She readily leaned down and pressed her mouth to his, marveling that even after a night spent in total misery he could still taste as fresh and sweet as a warm spring rain. Butterflies took wing in her stomach, as they always did when she was this close to him, whether from nervousness, desire, passion—or a combination of them all—and she deepened the kiss with a gentle sigh.

Even though he was bound, Nikolai fully participated in the embrace, first nibbling at her lips with his, then slipping his tongue sensually into her mouth with a lazy skill that curled her toes and stole away her senses. She braced her hands on the broad expanse of his chest and rested more of her weight on him, compelled by the bond between them, which was growing more and more strong as each moment passed, to be as close to him as possible no matter the consequences. A deep rumble of pleasure sounded from within him, letting her know without a doubt that he was just as affected by their closeness as she was.

Julia felt the sharp scrape of his elongated teeth and pulled back nervously to look at him. His eyes were glittering with their strange phosphorescent shimmer and she was shocked to note that the shape of his pupils had changed noticeably since their kiss began. Instead of round and black within the glittering ice of his irises they were now long, thin slivers that had an iridescent reflecting quality like those of an animal.

"What is it?" His voice was gruff with passion, or what she *hoped* was passion and not…something else.

"Your eyes," she told him hesitantly. "They're different.

His lids lowered, as if to hide those eyes from her. "How so?"

"You know how," she said. "They've changed."

"Do they frighten you?" he asked after a long moment of uneasy silence.

"A little. Should I back away now? Am I making you uncomfortable?" The last was a whisper as she felt a thrill of fear.

"No, not at all. In fact, I feel…calm. Excited," he chuckled and shifted in such a way that Julia had no doubts about just how excited he was, "but calm."

"What is happening to you, Nikolai?"

"I am not certain. All I know is that I have never been so out of touch with my own discipline as I have been these past few days. My feeling trapped in the confines of this city must be the reason why. I will have to leave for my home sooner than I had hoped."

"You can't leave now. You're not well enough." She left the thought unsaid that she couldn't bear to part from him so soon. That she was growing to care for him so strongly that were he to leave she would surely pine for his return. She didn't want to overburden him with her own sudden insecurities.

"I know you are right, but I cannot stay here. I cannot keep putting you at risk."

"I've been more afraid of you hurting yourself these past several hours, than of you hurting me. I don't think you give yourself enough credit. You haven't hurt me yet. I don't think you will."

"But what if you are wrong and I do something terrible?" he asked in a hoarse whisper. "That I could not bear."

Julia left her chair and crawled onto him in the bed, straddling his waist. She kept eye contact with him, seeing the sudden flare of his strange pupils as he intently watched her movements. "You're incredibly sexy, lying there all tied up like some kind of sacrificial offering."

"Julia. You are playing with fire," he warned.

"I know and it's *sooo* much fun." She ran her hands teasingly down the planes of his chest and stomach. She couldn't believe her own daring and knew that he was surprised by it as well. His body tightened beneath her, but she felt no nervousness, no fear that he was a wild thing—a werewolf—and might hurt her. In fact, that bit of danger only added a new spice to her desire for him. It only made her want him more. "I hope I don't get burned," she teased, roving her hands all over him now.

"Do not play with me, Julia. I am not myself."

"Don't you want me, Nikolai?" she asked breathlessly. That hidden, daring woman that had been awakened by him so many times before was now taking control of her better judgment and she had to admit that it felt wonderful.

"Of course I want you," he rasped. "I have never wanted anything more. But—"

"Shh! No buts. Let me give you pleasure, Nikolai. Don't worry about hurting me. You've been thrashing all night and you haven't broken free of your bonds yet. If you really want me to stop I will, otherwise lie back and let me love you. Let me give you pleasure. Let me help to make you happy, to forget your troubles for a little while."

Julia leaned down and kissed his chin, throat and collarbone. Gradually he eased beneath her and sighed as she caressed him. She stayed gentle, realizing how tired his muscles must be after his night of tossing and turning against the ties that bound him to the bed. She wanted to make his body sing with pleasure. She wanted to give him a release that he would remember for the rest of his life, no matter what happened between them. He was weak now, not himself, and at her mercy. And his vulnerability called to her on an elemental and primal level. In that moment all that mattered to her was his ultimate satisfaction and happiness. She couldn't help him with his strange illness, but was certain that she could help him to forget about it for a short while. Perhaps that would ease his suffering more than anything else could for the moment.

Julia hoped so.

Raising her arms, slowly for the greater benefit of his viewing pleasure, she removed her shirt. Her bra, a lacy pink confection that caused his eyes to widen and blaze with their appreciation, immediately followed. Her nipples were already hard little pebbles that unerringly drew his eyes. Curving her lips in a siren's smile she cupped her own breasts in her hands and plumped and squeezed them until his breath sounded in ragged, hungry bursts. His cock was marble hard against her sex and it was plain to see in the dark look on his face that her efforts pleased him mightily. She licked her fingers and moistened her nipples, then rolled them, as she knew he would have done had he been able to. Nikolai moaned and moved his hips more tightly into the cradle of her thighs—the only movement that his body was really capable of.

"You have amazing breasts, Julia. And your nipples are tender and delicious."

"Really?" she asked, then lifted her breast to her mouth and darted her tongue out to taste of them herself, pleased beyond measure when he groaned and clenched beneath her at the erotic sight. "I don't know if I agree about that, but I'm glad that you think so." Her voice was a husky whisper.

"I do. But the memory fades," he said dramatically. "Let me taste them again so that I can be sure." His eyes were devilish and wicked.

Julia leaned down, torturing him with the slow progress of her descent, and fitted her nipple against his waiting mouth. He latched onto her like a hungry babe, suckling her flesh until it tingled and swelled between his burning lips. She moaned and shifted against him so that her hair fell down over them both, a living curtain that served to shield and enclose them in their own private, golden haven.

Nikolai's mouth released her nipple with a loud, wet pop. His face was close to hers and his eyes were so beautiful at this proximity that she trembled with emotion. "Surely you have the tastiest nipples of all the women in all the world. Let me taste the other," he begged prettily.

Julia let him have his way, moaning as he drew her in again and loved her with his tireless mouth.

"Oh, Nikolai," she breathed. "You feel so good."

"So do you," he said, then his long tongue lapped out at her, laving her nipple until it glistened and tightened even further.

"Let me get my pants off," she whispered.

"Are you sure you trust me enough to do this?" he asked, giving her one last chance to back away from her chosen course.

"I trust you more than I've ever trusted anyone else, Nikolai," she assured him.

"Then undress. Quickly. I have a great need to be inside of you. Now."

Chapter Twelve

ꕥ

Even though it had only been one day since they'd last made love, it felt like a much longer time had passed to Julia. She was just as hungry for Nikolai as he was for her and an empty ache began to throb between her legs as she divested herself of her clothing. She was eager to join him on the bed again. Once again she was conscious of his eyes on her, following her every movement, so she made sure to please him by making a great show of her motions.

Her eyes strayed down to the demanding jut of his cock as it strained up towards the ceiling. Goodness, but he was truly magnificent! She couldn't help but admire him with her eyes and heart. With the body of a god, even while bound, and a disposition to match, it was no wonder that he was a dominant male within his society. Julia realized that he would never be tamed, never be conquered, and felt her heart swell with a fierce pride at the knowledge. He was perfect.

Julia crawled back over him, feeling the wet heat between her legs flood with readiness for his body's penetration of hers. His body was hot, but not with the fever that had raged through him during the long night. No, this was a different, purely erotic heat brought about by his fierce arousal, she knew. He shifted beneath her as much as he was able to and his cock butted against the swelling bud of her clit, making her gasp and jerk her hips in response. She spread her legs wider and rocked her slippery arousal against him, until he was panting with each velvet slide of her body.

Her hands kneaded the bulging muscles of his chest, feeling them roll and bunch as Nikolai shifted. His stomach muscles were firm and delineated, like a washboard of living tissue, disappearing into the dark hair on his pubis that peeked out at her between her legs as she rocked over him. The breathtaking, masculine sight he presented made her breath catch in her throat while looking at him.

She leaned down to kiss him and was pleasantly surprised at the wild ferociousness of his response. His tongue speared into her mouth over and over again, and his teeth scraped against hers, mashing their lips so tightly together that her mouth was soon swollen and throbbing against his.

As she slid her body over his she caressed his chest and belly with her hands, and as she pulled back from their hungry kiss to gain a breath she couldn't help but lave his soft, full lips with her tongue, savoring his taste. Julia couldn't get enough of him, she wanted to devour him whole so strong was her attraction to him. And knowing that he was tied beneath her, completely at her mercy, only made her want him more. She felt dominant…yet still strangely dominated because she couldn't for the life of her resist his potent allure—not even enough to pull back and slow their pace, though she knew it was probably wisest to do so. For his sake as much as hers.

"Are you up to this, truly?" she asked against his mouth, in between long, deep kisses.

"Yes. Yes a million times," he vowed moments later, moving beneath her as much as he was able, pressing their sexes together erotically.

"I need you so much. I don't know what's come over me," she moaned.

"You are my mate, Julia. It is right that you need me this way. I need you, too, more than I know how to say in any language."

"I'm not pretty," she gasped in between kisses, sounding apologetic for her own flaws.

"You are so beautiful you make my heart ache," he said into her mouth.

"I'm not worldly."

"Your innocence only makes me want to protect you all the more," he promised, then licked the roof of her mouth, as their kisses grew deeper and deeper still.

"You've probably been with tons more women who were better in bed than me." It hurt more than she would have guessed to realize that.

"I've never been with any other woman. Only you."

Julia pulled back from his mouth in surprise. "You're lying," she scoffed, not believing him for a second.

"Julia." His voice was soft but utterly serious and the look in his eyes made her insides turn to liquid. "Wolves mate for life, and werewolves are much the same. I have had my duty to my pack and my homeland to keep me company while I was waiting for you. I had no need to find a bedmate, knowing that in time I would find you. You were all I ever needed, Julia fair. Julia, my mate."

"Then you were a virgin the other night? Like me?" she asked, finding the idea much to her liking.

"No other woman but you would have fulfilled me in any way, so there was no point in trying. Until you I needed only to use my hand to find physical release. With you I find my release spiritually as well as physically and it has been worth all my years of waiting and abstaining."

"Oh, *Nikolai*." She wanted to tell him that she loved him and that she never wanted to be parted from him. But Julia had never said such things to anyone before and couldn't find the right words to convey the depth of the emotions she was feeling. So she kissed him and put as much of her love and as much of her passion into that embrace as she could manage, hoping he would understand and know at least some of what she was feeling. Julia wanted him to feel that, in her arms and heart, he would find a mate worthy of an alpha werewolf.

But first she had to overcome her own self-doubt—no easy task by any stretch of her imagination—and prove to herself her own worth. Thankfully this was the perfect opportunity for that. Nikolai was bound and at her mercy, leaving this encounter open for her to choreograph as she pleased. This was her opportunity to push his limits and prove to them both that she could handle whatever he dished out in response. No matter what that response was.

Julia pulled back and gave him a devilish smile. Never taking her eyes from his, she crawled slowly down his body until she rested at the foot of the bed. Her hands were trembling slightly as she ran them over the strong planes of his large feet—not in fear, but in desire—as she marveled at how such masculine feet could manage to look so sinfully attractive as well. His toes curled when she ran the backs of her hands over the soles, and he chuckled.

Her werewolf was ticklish!

Julia couldn't resist taking advantage of that knowledge by raking her nails lightly back and forth over his sensitive skin. Soon Nikolai was gritting his fanged teeth against his deep laughter, trying valiantly not to show how affected he was by such teasing. Julia found it incredibly endearing and just when she knew her teasing had become too much for him she stroked over his feet, soothing them, and progressed upwards to his calves. They were covered in fair, golden hair, which was soft and slightly crisp to the touch, making her want to burrow her face against him. And why not, she thought? Why not give in to the temptation? She knew instinctively that nothing would be forbidden her in regards to Nikolai's body. So she gave in to the impulse and rubbed her face against the fur of his legs, reveling in the feel of it against her skin.

His body was absolute perfection. Over and over she had marveled at his masculine appeal, but now more than ever she could see the effects his change was having on his form and realized that he was growing impossibly more and more beautiful as his transformation progressed. He was quite noticeably more massive and heavily muscled. His shoulders, which always seemed broad, were now close to spanning the mattress of her bed. Julia couldn't help but feel a thrill, wondering just how strong he might be now, beneath her. Thankfully he didn't seem strong enough to break through his bonds.

Yet. She shivered deliciously at the thought.

Julia moved up, scattering butterfly kisses across his knees, one after the other. Goodness, she even loved his knees! His thighs called to her next, of course, those muscled columns that were as thick as tree trunks. She tested and kneaded at the hard ridges there with her hands and mouth, impassioned by the strong feel of him. She was growing hotter and wetter as she explored him, becoming breathless with anticipation for yet more.

The perfumed scent of his sex called to her unmercifully. He smelled like the deep forest, piney, woodsy, crisp and delicious. And Julia knew, instinctively, that he smelled nothing at all like a human male would. The gently curling, golden hair that fleeced his testicles glinted in the sunlight, immediately drawing her eyes to it. His testicles were heavy but tightly drawn against his body. His cock was thick, as big around as her wrist, and long, reaching up beyond his belly button in his fiercely aroused state. Giving in to a compulsion that would have otherwise embarrassed her had she stopped to give it any thought, she leaned down and nuzzled her face into the splayed vee of his thighs. He smelled heavenly and felt better yet.

Julia rubbed her face against his testes, licking and kissing his sensitive tissues with shameless abandon. Nikolai moaned and shifted against her rooting face, trembling with the force of his own arousal. She drew the hard spheres of his sac into her mouth, gently sucking on him, and he nearly managed to buck her off so violently did he move in response.

"Julia, that feels so *goooooood*," he howled. The unmistakably canine sound startled but excited her, and she took more of him into her mouth, as much as she could fit without hurting him.

All the while she suckled him, her hands roved over his body, exploring the liquid ripples of the muscles in his stomach and chest as he moved beneath her. He was a delight of poetic motion beneath her fingertips, amazing her with every tiny nuance of movement that he made. He didn't move like a normal person—like a *human*—his musculature seemed much more in nature complex than that. He looked like a human but he moved like a dream. She'd always noticed that about him, but never more than she did now when he was at her mercy on the bed. His body was truly an amazing construction of muscle and bone, a miracle in evolutionary design.

She wanted to paint him. Or sculpt him. Or better yet, both. His perfection had to be captured in art, *her* art, to pay homage to it properly in her estimation.

"I need to be inside of you, my Julia. You are driving me mad with lust," Nikolai groaned.

Julia noticed how he strained at his bonds, not in fevered delirium now as he had only hours before, but in passionate response to her caresses. She drew her mouth away from his testicles and smiled up at him. She darted her tongue out and licked along the shaft of his penis as though it were an ice cream cone. Nikolai roared his response and jerked beneath her again.

"Do not toy with me, Julia. I can smell how ready you are, you do not need to be more prepared to take me into your body. Stop teasing me," he demanded.

She ignored him, popped the head of his cock into her mouth and suckled on it as though it were a lollipop. He bucked his hips and sent his shaft deeper into her mouth. She coated his length with the moisture of her own saliva and moved on him in a rhythm she knew he would like best. Up and down, down and up she moved, taking him over and over again into the hot cave of her throat. He was absolutely delicious!

Julia heard a cracking, splintering sound and jerked her mouth away from him to see what the racket was. Gasping, she witnessed Nikolai's hands, now sporting long, wicked claws, digging into the wood of her bed frame as he hung on for dear life. Deep, ragged scars riddled the wood where his claws had scraped before finding purchase, accounting for the startling noise.

"Please, Julia. Take me," he growled, shamelessly begging her for release.

It thrilled her to no end that she had brought this response from him with her ministrations. She bestowed one last tonguing kiss to the crown of his sex and crawled further up his body. "Since you asked so nicely, I guess I'll give in just this once," she teased in a whisper.

"Minx. You will pay for this when I am free." His dark smile was a wicked promise all its own.

"Who says I'll ever untie you after such a threat?"

"Oh, I promise you that I will make it an enjoyable debt to fulfill. Never doubt that, love." He snapped his fanged jaws threateningly, but his eyes twinkled with devilish enjoyment. "Now wrap that lovely pussy of yours around my cock and fuck me hard like I know you want to."

His base words thrilled her to her toes and she moved to do just that. She was so wet between her legs that when she straddled him she looked down to see one lone, silvery drop of her arousal splash down onto his heated flesh. He gasped, obviously having felt it, and groaned. Julia slowly lowered herself onto him, tentative in her movements, as this position was new for her. The broad tip of his cock butted against her portal and Julia felt a small resistance then a tiny pop as he slid into her, stretching her. She let out a shuddering breath as she lowered herself, slowly, onto him. It seemed to take forever, but at last she was seated fully upon him, feeling him deep within her as never before.

"You feel like silk and fire, gripping me like a fist. I can feel your heart beat around me, pulsing in rhythm to mine. I have never felt such bliss," he moaned out.

Julia was beyond words, beyond thought, beyond anything but *feeling*. She leaned forward and braced her hands on his chest, taking him impossibly deeper into her body, and kissed him with all the pent up passion she'd been hoarding over the course of her life. She lifted her hips up off of him, until his cock had almost slipped free of her, then lowered back onto him. Slowly she repeated the movements, sheathing him again and again in her wet heat, the friction caused by her movements driving them both up towards the heavens.

Nikolai's sharpened teeth bit into the soft flesh of her lower lip as their kisses grew deeper and more impassioned. The small bite was just short of breaking the skin and made her cry out with surprise at the mixture of pleasure and pain the tiny nip caused.

"Sorry," he murmured before their kisses resumed once more and she responded by rolling her hips over him in a sensuous, feline movement, drawing a gasp of pleasure from Nikolai and swallowing it greedily into her mouth. She repeated the movement and he groaned. It thrilled her to her toes that she could affect him so dramatically with nothing but the motions of her body and his responses encouraged her to use her body upon him more creatively, swaying and rolling, grinding and thrusting onto him, using her breasts and belly and legs to caress him as she moved. It was decadent. It was wonderful and they were both soon breathless and moaning with passionate abandon, heedless to the symphony of noises they made between them.

Julia increased her rhythm as her body wound itself tight in preparation for release and Nikolai hissed between his teeth as his climax approached in unison with hers. Moving her body just so, she angled her hips down so that Nikolai's pubic hair rubbed deliciously against her swollen clit. The gentle, scraping friction against her most sensitive tissue made her gasp and moan and dig her fingers into the muscles of his chest as she rode him. Nikolai roared and bucked up against her so violently that there came a great cracking noise—the protestations of splintering wood—and suddenly he had his arms free of their bonds.

"Oh god," Julia cried, in surprise to see her bed frame decimated and in pleasant shock as her body clamped itself down on and around Nikolai's when she came.

It was a wondrous release and so all consuming that Julia's vision and hearing dimmed so that all that remained in her world was the feel, taste and smell of Nikolai. And the sound—he roared loud enough to alarm the entire apartment building surely—as he rose up beneath her and reached out his arms to clutch her tightly to him.

There came a white-hot pain at her shoulder and she cried out with the unexpectedness of it, but she was so far gone in her release that the pain only mingled with the pleasure, driving her up higher and higher into the stars. Never before had there been such exquisite ecstasy, such mindless bliss. Had Julia tried she would never have been able to explain the wonder that she felt just then. Colors of unimagined hue danced behind her tightly closed eyelids. Perfumed scents of a thousand different unknown hosts assailed her nostrils, until her head swam with more than just sexual delight. Her hearing came back with a rush and a roar, and Julia would have sworn that she could hear the slightest whisper of the mice in the building, the steady drone and hum of electric gadgets throughout the city, the honk and brake of the cars in the streets beyond her apartment.

Nikolai's mouth was at her shoulder, holding her as only a dominant male would as he thrust into her, spending himself with a hot rush of semen into her womb. Even that sense, that feeling of his body filling hers, was magnified to the point that it seemed to Julia she could feel every separate drop of his essence as it flowed into her. It was magnificent in every way imaginable, like nothing Julia had ever known before, and she screamed out her joy, clutching her lover to her as tightly as she could manage with desperate hands. The scent of him filled her, drowning out all the other strange smells that had bombarded her, and her heart ached with the need for more of that perfect bouquet. She wanted to roll her body in that scent—to mark herself with his essence—so that his memory would never be far from her mind. So that any who dared to stray too close would know she belonged to him wholly and utterly, in every way.

It was madness. It was chaos. It was love.

Eons seemed to pass them by, ages in which they shuddered and moaned and spent themselves in each other's embrace. Then their passions abated and they were left in the afterglow. Trembling with a sudden and great fatigue, they collapsed back against the pillows and the bed, much abused these past two days, and fell with a mighty thud onto the floor. The frame fell in tatters about them, but they were by far too weary to give it much notice. Julia felt warm moisture at her shoulder and reached a lazy hand up to find that Nikolai had broken her skin with his bite, leaving tiny rivulets of blood behind. The wound burned but did not pain her over much so she let it go, snuggling down into her lover's arms and letting her heavy eyes close.

Within moments they were both heavily asleep, ensconced more deeply in Morpheus' embrace than ever they had been before, so weary were they. And, unnoticed, the punctures in Julia's flesh—caused by Nikolai's wolfish fangs—closed slowly until the bleeding stopped.

Chapter Thirteen

ꟼ

It was late afternoon when Julia awoke from her slumber. Nikolai was still deeply asleep, looking so handsome and young in his repose that Julia's breath was stolen from her at the sight. His face was completely free of care and worry and it was the first time Julia had ever seen it thus. It warmed her heart to know that she had helped him find such peace.

Looking about her she chuckled at the disarray that littered the floor about them. Strangely enough, the sight of her poor, abused bed didn't upset her in the least. Though she didn't have the funds to replace her bed frame it didn't seem to matter much just then. There were more important things on her mind.

Like food.

Her stomach was empty and aching, growling and snarling its discomfort so loudly that Julia was surprised the noise didn't wake Nikolai. But he slept on, obviously needing his rest far more than food just then. She rolled from the mattress as it rested in dishevelment on the floor and shot to her feet with a giggle. She felt invigorated, happy and ready to face the world. Skipping to the kitchen she looked in her cupboards and refrigerator for something suitable—or at least something filling—to eat. All that she found was her customary stash of ramen noodles, canned soup, crackers and bread. She supposed she could whip up a quick mayonnaise sandwich—the pauper's delicacy she'd adopted as her own in recent years—it would tide her over until Nikolai awakened and she could make more soup for the both of them then.

It took her no more than a minute to make her meal—two pieces of bread, mayonnaise, salt and pepper—and even less time than that to devour it. She looked at the time and went to make a phone call. She planned on playing hooky from work, the first time ever for her.

George picked up on the fifth ring.

"Hello Georgie, pordgie," Julia quipped.

"Julia? You sound really weird."

"Yeah, well thanks for being tactful." Julia laughed at her own upbeat tone. It was truly good to be alive. "Remember Friday when you said you'd cover for me whatever day I wanted if I would fill in for your shift?" She didn't give him any time to answer before she barreled onward. "Well guess what, Georgie? Today's that day—or tonight, I guess I should say. I'm scheduled from seven p.m. until three a.m. and I'll need you to fill in for me."

"Wait a minute, Julia, I can't—"

"Sorry, George, but I gotta go now. Be sure you're there on time. If you're not...well lets just say that your mommy and daddy will have to send you more spending money because you certainly won't be earning it at the hotel."

"You can't fire me, Julia. You don't have that authority," George scoffed.

"Maybe not, but Mr. Morlock certainly does. And when I threaten to quit if you're not booted out, who do you think he'll send packing?"

"That's not fair," George whined.

"So sorry, so sad, boo hoo hoo." Julia laughed at herself again, surprised at her own behavior but reveling in it all the same. It was amazing what a bout of good sex could do for one's self-confidence. "Be at work or else, George. Bye, bye." She hung up on his sputtered protestations, feeling rather pleased with herself.

Julia went into her bedroom once more to check on Nikolai. He seemed to be resting deeply and calmly; all of the previous night's rages seemed to have left him. Perhaps his fears were unfounded and his change wasn't upon him just yet, or perhaps he was becoming more accustomed to the city around him. Julia couldn't guess. But she was glad that he seemed more at ease just now. The question was, would he stay this way? Or would his agitation return once he awakened from his slumber? It was probably better that she err on the side of caution and go out to buy more rope, just in case he needed to be tied up once more. The bed was a shambles so she couldn't tie him to it should the need arise, but if she bought enough rope she could perhaps hog-tie him until he got better. Surely that would hold him, no matter how strong he was.

Julia quickly penned a note to Nikolai, telling him she would be out for an hour or so—in case he awoke while she was out purchasing necessary supplies—and left it for him on the pillow beside his head. She couldn't resist running her fingers lightly over his golden hair as it spilled out around him. It felt like the softest of silks and glinted in the sunlight that spilled through her bedroom windows. She could have stood there for hours, just watching him sleep, but she had errands to run. She forced herself to back away from her lover, exiting the room and closing the door with a soft click behind her, leaving Nikolai to his rest.

* * * * *

New York City was a bustling giant of a place. Even in the worst weather the sidewalks were crowded with people, and on a busy day when viewed from the high windows above, the ground below seemed to undulate like a giant serpent with the movement of so many bodies. Julia had never grown used to the massive numbers of people that surrounded her day by day, having been raised in a small and lightly populated area. She was more accustomed to wide, open spaces, with barely a soul wandering about at any given time. Crowds were not her cup of tea, to say the very least.

But today nothing could have blackened her good mood. Which was good because it was a lovely afternoon and many people had ventured out of doors to enjoy it. Instead of hiring a cab to take her to the nearest hardware store, Julia elected to walk the several blocks herself, the better to savor such a fine day. It was easy to forget, amidst such pollution and noise, that there were still some vestiges of nature's bounty to be found on the city streets. Small, kept flowerbeds abounded, along with the occasional fenced off tree. Pigeons were forever in abundance here, but sometimes if one was lucky, one could catch a glimpse of a blue jay, sparrow, or starling. Today, Julia was exceptionally lucky indeed, for a bright red cardinal caught her eye as she passed a small oak tree.

The bird fascinated her, as the sunlight caught the bright plumage and cast brilliant rainbows about the tiny animal. Julia had to shield her eyes against the wondrous color, but she dare not look away for fear that the bird would take flight before she could savor the moment properly. The bird hopped around, searching for insects in the bark of the young tree, puffing its little chest out proudly when it found a mite or two and gobbled it down. Julia would have sworn that she could see the trembling of the bird's heartbeat within its breast as it pounded there, so intently did she study it. What a beautiful bird it was. How wondrous it seemed that she should catch sight of it on this happy day.

A car horn blared into the air, causing both Julia and the foraging cardinal to jump in startled surprise at the grating sound. The bird took wing into the air, its rouge feathers tinged with gold as the sun shone through, but Julia wasn't ready to say farewell to the bird just yet. She raced after it, heedless of the impulsiveness of such an action, or the stares that she received from the passersby as she ran through the crowded walkways. The bird landed on a small fence railing a little over a block away. Julia slowly approached, entranced by the sight of it as it cleaned its feathers, unfazed after its flight from the noises of the surrounding humans.

How much time passed, Julia didn't know, but she was content to stand there and study the bird, following it when it flew off to find other perches, her mind calmed and eased by so simple a thing. The afternoon sun sank low on the horizon, and the concrete beneath her feet cooled somewhat, drawing her back to herself with a jolt. She remembered her purpose, looked around with some chagrin to find herself several blocks off her original course. She would have to hail that cab after all, if she were to return in a timely manner to Nikolai. She stepped into the street and waved down a passing yellow cab, climbed into the backseat and gave her destination to the driver.

Less than ten minutes later she was entering the hardware store, in search of a length of rope or chain that might be strong enough to hold Nikolai at bay should he grow agitated during the night ahead.

"Do you need any help miss?" A young salesman had approached her as she searched through the aisles.

"I need several feet of heavy rope or chain, if you have any," she replied.

The young man smiled, appearing more than eager to help her. "We do. Follow me and I can measure out a length of heavy chain and cut it for you. Do you have a dog you want to chain outside or something?" he asked conversationally.

"Something like that. I need it to tie a wolf to my bed." Julia found her words beyond funny and roared with laughter, heedless that the salesman might think her unhinged. "Or you could even say I have my own pet monster to subdue."

But the man didn't seem to be paying her much heed, even though he was staring at her quite intently. He quickly led her to another aisle where he measured out several feet of chain that was as thick around as her wrist and used bolt cutters to sever the end from the large coiled dispenser. Julia reached for the chain but the man was adamant about carrying it up to the front registers for her, remarking that it was quite a heavy burden for her to bear.

"Thanks," Julia responded politely.

"You know…I probably shouldn't say this, seeing as how I'm at work but…you have the most lovely hair I've ever seen." The young man blushed at his own forwardness.

Julia couldn't have been more stunned had the man reached out and punched her in the face. She didn't often receive compliments and was surprised to receive one now, considering the fact that she hadn't even showered. "Er, thank you. That's very kind of you to say." At least she wasn't stuttering, as she was often wont to do around guys in situations like this.

"Not kind at all, it's the truth. Umm…I was wondering…" The man shuffled his feet, seeming nervous and unsure of himself. "Would you like to go out to dinner tonight?" The man ended in a rush.

Julia knew her eyes had to be the size of golf balls in her face as she looked at him. "Well, thank you for the offer but I'm kind of in a relationship right now. Maybe some other time," she said, not knowing what else to say after the unexpected offer.

"Any time you want," the man exclaimed. "Here, let me give you my number. Call anytime you want, whenever you want. We can go out and catch a film or some dinner or…something." The man quickly scribbled his number on a scrap piece of paper he found in his apron pocket and handed it to her. Julia took it with a wane smile and put it in her purse. A few minutes later she had paid for her length of chain and was back in a cab on her way towards home.

It had been one of the nicest, and also one of the strangest outings since she'd moved to the city. She couldn't help but smile with anticipation as her conveyance took her to her home. Perhaps the night would be just as pleasant as the afternoon had been. With Nikolai waiting for her, she had high hopes that it would be.

* * * * *

Julia entered her apartment with the chain swinging over her shoulder. She laid her burden—it hadn't been *that* heavy—on her couch and tiptoed quietly to her bedroom door. She poked her head through to get a peek at Nikolai, to see if he was still sleeping, but he wasn't in the bed.

"Nikolai?" she called, moving to the bathroom in search of him. "Are you in there?" she asked through the closed door. She knocked, waited, and when there was no answer she knocked again. "Nikolai?" She opened the door.

The bathroom was empty.

Julia felt a stirring of anxiety and wandered about the apartment in search of him. He was nowhere to be found. She went back into the bedroom searching for a note from him—maybe he'd gone out for food, not finding anything palatable in her cupboards—but there was nothing. Not a sign. Nikolai's clothing and belongings were gone as well.

Had he simply forgotten to leave her a note? She looked again to be sure there wasn't one and heaved a sigh when her search proved fruitless. Worry took hold in her heart. What if he'd relapsed and gone into another rage and left? What if he had decided to seek a doctor's care after all?

What if he'd left to return to his homeland?

So many questions without answer assailed her. What was there for her to do? She went into the kitchen, picked up her phone, and dialed the number for the hotel. George answered the phone, sounding bored and rude as always, and she promptly asked for Nikolai's room, speaking quickly so that George wouldn't be given the time to recognize her voice.

The phone in Nikolai's room rang again and again and again, until George answered again and asked for her to leave a message. She hung up on his request and bit her lip in consternation.

Where was he?

Just then, something caught the corner of her eye. A small envelope of folded notebook paper was taped to her refrigerator door and she snatched at it in a flurry. The contents of the letter made her cry out in dismay and caused her eyes to flood with tears, which in turn spilled down over her cheeks.

My dearest and most fair Julia,

Forgive me for leaving you like this but I fear that you are no longer safe with me. I did the unspeakable and inflicted harm upon you this morning. In my passion I lost control, destroyed your bed and bit into your tender flesh. Please forgive me, I beg of you. There is no excuse for my behavior, nor do I seek to give one. More than anything, I wish that I could change what I am and live with you as a human, but alas I cannot. I must leave you now, until I am more myself. Know that, above all, I love you. And no matter what happens, you will always be my one, my only, my mate.

Forever,

Nikolai

Along with the note was a check written out to her in the sum of fifteen thousand dollars—a king's ransom and no mistake in her mind—for the replacement of her bed. A bed that had cost her less than two hundred dollars at a second hand store. Julia sank down onto the floor, clutching the note to her chest and cried in deep racking sobs, feeling as if her very heart had been broken.

She feared she would never see him again. And she hadn't even told him she loved him. Now she would never get the chance. Damn her for a coward.

And damn Nikolai as well.

Chapter Fourteen

ꟗ

Nikolai wandered about the expanse of Central Park, seeing nothing, hearing nothing, lost deeply within his own thoughts. His mind tortured him with visions of Julia's flesh, torn and bloody after he had sunk his fangs into her. Of the utter devastation he'd visited upon her bed, leaving it in tatters around them. How could he have lost control so completely? How could he have placed her in such danger, willingly and eagerly, simply because he so desired to be near her? He was a fool and a disgrace, unworthy of the title of alpha.

He could have killed her.

It mattered less than nothing to him that he had refrained from harming her further. It was the principle of the thing. She could have died by his own traitorous hands, no matter how honorable his intentions might have been. He felt like a monster. She had nursed him, forgiven him his bad tempered treatment of her and loved him despite his wolfish state. He didn't deserve one so noble and pure of heart as Julia. He should have stayed away from her the moment he realized something was wrong with his cycle, should have protected her from himself at all costs. But he was a selfish beast. He had wanted so desperately to be near her, to love her physically and spiritually, that his good sense had flown from him utterly. He had willingly placed her in danger and must never do so again.

But already he missed her. Already he hungered to be near her again, to see her face, smell her sweet scent and hold her in his arms. It was madness, this. To have such an all-consuming ache to be with her, to pine for her as he would for food or water. It alarmed him, this need he had of her—he who had never needed anyone but himself. He couldn't begin to understand it.

One thing was for certain. He couldn't bring himself to leave her and return, alone, to his homeland. The very thought of doing so, of leaving without her, sent him into an instinctive and desperate panic. And yet, he could not stay with her—to do so could put her at a very grave risk—he dare not trust himself to keep his wild instincts at bay around her. So what other choice was left to him? Go or stay, both options were unacceptable to him.

If only things could be different between them. If only he could trust himself to love her without hurting her. All he wanted in life was to be with her. Julia, his one and only true mate.

Perhaps Ivan or Brianna would have the answers for him. They were the only inter-species mated pair in their race's memory. Surely they would have some insight into this dilemma—perhaps they had faced the same choices he now faced—surely they could help him. He would call them at the soonest opportunity. Ivan was one of the few of them with generated electric power—a wedding present to his mate, who was used to such conveniences—and he had a satellite telephone. Ivan would have advice for him, surely.

For the first time in Nikolai's life, he sought out help from his brethren, more than willing to humble himself before a lesser member of his pack in doing so. Anything for Julia.

Anything.

* * * * *

"You are sure you never felt this way with Brianna, Ivan?"

"At first I feared for her safety, of course. I have never interacted much with humans and wasn't sure how to with her, but I never felt the rages you have described. I never felt the urge to attack Bri."

"I never wished to attack Julia either, cousin. But I did."

"But you did not harm her overmuch, by your own admission. She felt well enough to venture out while you slept. Perhaps you have overreacted, misjudged the situation."

"I could have killed her, Ivan. The fact that I did not gives me great comfort, I assure you, but only that. There is always a chance that I could harm her further. There is always a chance that she could *die*."

"And so it is the same with Bri and myself. I am by far stronger than she. At any given moment I could tear her limb from limb. But I do not. I am not a slave to my baser instincts…and neither are you. You are far more noble and strong than I. If you tell yourself you will not harm this woman—your mate—then you must have faith in your ability to restrain yourself."

"I drew blood from her, Ivan," Nikolai admitted in a hushed murmur.

"It was an accident, Niki. These things happen. Humans are frail creatures in body. But it is their strength of spirit that makes them a match for us as mates. Their courageous hearts see them through the most difficult of challenges. Julia will be no exception. Go to her. Tell her your worries. Let her make the choice for you. It is as much her decision to make as it is yours."

"She will chose to stay with me, I know it. I cannot put her at such risk, she does not understand the cost."

Ivan sighed deeply on the other end of the line. "Love is risk. The greatest risk of all. And I know you, Niki, perhaps better than you do right now in your turmoil. You have never worried about risks so long as the prize was worth winning. Is Julia not worth winning? Is she not worth the risk?"

"I know you are trying to bolster my spirits, cousin. I am grateful, doubt it not. But this is not so simple a thing as a hunt or a race among pact mates. This is far more serious. I love Julia, more than anything. And that is why I must stay as far away from her as possible."

"I know that you will do what you feel is best. But I implore you to think on it further before you make a decision. The full moon isn't for another fortnight, so you still have time before the change to join with your mate and bring her here should you chose that path. We are fine here without you. Take all the time you need."

"Thank you Ivan. Give my love to Brianna."

"Take care of yourself, my alpha. And your mate as well."

Nikolai hung up the phone and turned his face up to the sky, wishing for rain to hide his tears, that he may weep freely as he so longed to do.

Several moments later his mournful howl echoed about the streets of the city.

Julia heard it in her broken, tear stained slumber and cried out his name in her empty apartment. It was a long and lonely night for both of them.

Chapter Fifteen

ꟷ

Three days had passed since Julia had last seen Nikolai and she was beyond weary of waiting for him. Every time her phone rang at home her heart began to pound with hope that it might be him. Every time a tall man approached the reception desk at work she did a double take and was disappointed when it wasn't Nikolai. Nikolai hadn't returned to his hotel room once in the past three days, not that it would have done him any good. Julia had removed his belongings and checked him out of the hotel the second night of his disappearance. Let him come looking for his things—he'd have to go through her to get them—maybe he'd apologize for his abandonment and beg for her forgiveness.

How hopeless the situation was! On the one hand Julia was so angry with him for worrying her that she could spit, but on the other hand she missed him so badly that she would have dispensed with her anger immediately for the smallest bit of news from him. Was he ok? Had his change become too much for him to bear, here in the city? Had he returned to Russia, to his family who might be able to help him through it? So many questions—all without answers—they were making her sick with fear and worry.

If only she had told him how she felt. That she loved him, needed him, and possibly couldn't live without him. Perhaps then he would have understood that this silence from him was hurting her far more than it was helping her. Nothing he could do to her physically in the rages of his change could hurt her like this. Her heart ached so much at times that she feared it would shatter in her chest.

She missed him, crazy as that might be after only knowing him a few days, but it was true. She missed him so much that she'd taken to sleeping with articles of his clothing, lying on the mattress that still sat on the floor of her apartment—she refused to cash his check, let him wonder what had become of it when his bank account reflected that the money was still there—snuggling with a shirt or sweater that still bore his woodsy masculine scent. It was a small comfort indeed, but it was all that she had to see her through the long lonely nights without him.

In her pocket she kept his note and check, the closest links she had with him now, touching them every now and again throughout the day to reassure herself in small measures.

At times during the day at school or work she unexpectedly caught faint vestiges of his scent and pined for his nearness with a physical yearning that was almost unbearable. His essence was burned into her nostrils, there when she least expected it, teasing her enough that she often caught herself looking around for him, hoping that he might be there waiting for her to notice him. But of course that never happened. He was probably hundreds of miles away by now, deep in his forest home.

He'd probably already forgotten her. Sure, he'd sworn his love for her, but no man could love as he said he did her and be able to leave like this with no word or contact for days. It was a horrible thing for Nikolai to have done, tease her with promises of love ever after, and then leave her without looking back. If she ever had the opportunity she would beat that fact home into his stubborn skull…just before she drowned him in kisses, demanding that he never leave her side again. She loved him. She nearly hated him. At times she wished she had never met him. And at others she was so grateful to have known him, to have loved and been loved by him, that she could have wept tears of joy. It was enough to drive her mad, being so at odds with herself.

But one good thing had come of her meeting Nikolai, at least. She now had an abundance of self-confidence that she'd never possessed before. It was helping her in her studies at school, not having so much self-doubt as she used to, as well as at work and in her private life—what little there was of it. At the hotel, Nora had even remarked on it, noting that she walked with shoulders straight and head held high, without stuttering or shying away from unfamiliar men whenever they strayed too close. It was something Julia hadn't dwelled too much on, but it was there just the same. She was surer of herself, more at ease in her own body, and less caring of what other people might think of her. It was a positive side-benefit to knowing Nikolai that Julia had never expected but appreciated all the same.

But she would have given that up, given anything at all, for some small bit of news from Nikolai. As the days wore on she began to suspect that Nikolai was gone from her. Forever.

Today, the third day after Nikolai's disappearance, Julia was free of work and school obligations, a rare occurrence and one she didn't wish to squander by lying around and worrying about her missing werewolf. Not that Nikolai was far from her thoughts, quite the opposite in fact. She was painting his portrait—a nude, of course—in oils. The piece was coming along with surprising ease, even for her. Her hand was unusually steady and rapid as she stroked the sable brush along the canvas. The animal smell of the brush was driving her to distraction, but she firmly pushed it away as best she could as she continued. Normally when she painted she used less graceful strokes, changing this or that in the composition of a piece until the paint was thick and heavily textured, but not today. Today she was supremely confident in her abilities.

Nikolai's features were nearly photographic as the image spilled from her mind onto the canvas. The strong arch of his black brow, the pouting curve of his sensuous lips and the exotic tilt of his cheekbones, nose and jaw were a spot on match. Colors of alizarin crimson, cobalt blue, mars black, cadmium yellow and ultramarine blue splashed across the piece, making it look vibrant, emotional and untamed. In fact, if Julia's eyes strayed too long from the piece she began to see it as an alien work. If she hadn't known for certain that the piece was hers and had in fact come from her own brush strokes, she would never have believed herself capable of such work. The technique was a new one to her, but one she found she quite liked.

Her strokes were broad and slashing, crisp but architectured with a purely artistic flair. The colors were bold, but blended well to create the desired effect. Nikolai's hair was her favorite feature of all, in life and on canvas. She had used ochre and yellow with white highlights for that, giving it a windblown look that she was quite proud of. For his golden tanned body she had used a mixture of raw sienna, ochre and the lightest touch of cobalt blue, with excess burnt sienna and cobalt blue for the dips and shadows of his form. His eyes were a mixture of ultramarine blue and white, blended just so to capture the silvery aquamarine of his irises. Just looking into them gave Julia the shivers, as if they were real.

The smell of the sable and hog bristle brushes that she was using permeated the air around her. Those animal hairs, mixed with the pungent smells of oils and turpentine, stung her nostrils more than she was accustomed to. She went to a window and opened it for more ventilation, pausing to breath deeply of the crisp outdoor air and watch the pigeons fly by on their daily errands.

She was doing that more and more often of late, watching the birds and the trees and the sky, all Nikolai's doing of course. Just spending those few precious days with him had given her a new appreciation of the world around her. She no longer bowed her head and rushed through the crowded streets of the city. Now she took her time, savoring the nuances of her surroundings, strolling instead of hurrying to each destination. She was a changed woman, in many ways.

Julia took a sumi brush—not intended for use with oils, but effective all the same—and used it for its unique effects in the finishing touches of her portrait. Surprisingly it hadn't taken her any time at all to perfect the piece, merely a few pleasant hours, instead of her customary several days. It would take a solid week to dry of course, because of her use of oils, but it would be well worth the wait to see the end product. Perhaps she could submit the work for extra credit at school. But then again perhaps not. Julia was finding more and more reasons to skimp out on her work at school.

As if school didn't matter any more.

After so many years of hard work and planning, Julia began to wonder if school just wasn't a waste of her time. Perhaps she was trying too hard to get by in school, when she should be trying to get by in life instead. She'd never given it much thought before, but now she began to wonder if her talents wouldn't be better served by submission into the open markets of the art world. So much of her money was spent on books and training through school...but wasn't true art the product of inspiration and true talent? Julia used to think so. She was beginning to think that way again.

What had she gained by going to school? Self-confidence? There was that. A future in the art world? Not necessarily. She could earn a degree and apply it towards teaching, but as far as being recognized as a great artist—as she'd always hoped and dreamed she would be—no school could give her that. She had to earn it on her own. Did the lessons at the school offer her training? Newfound skills? She had learned much since enrolling, true. But as far as honing her techniques and adopting new habits with her work, she'd learned more about this through Nikolai's vision of the world than she'd learned her whole life on her own or at school.

Perhaps it was time for her to take a chance, to find an agent and begin circulating her works beyond her own doors or those of the classroom. Much had changed in the past week.

She had changed. Her art had changed. Everything was different now.

Julia cleaned her brushes, carefully removing all traces of paint from the bristles as she'd always done, curling her lip against the pungent odor of the turpentine as it wafted up into her sensitive nostrils. Then, beneath the smells of her workspace she caught a whiff of Nikolai…again.

How long would it take for her to get over the scent of him—the memory of him? Would she look for him around every street corner, in every tall man's face as he walked by her? These questions had been plaguing her ceaselessly for the past four days and she was still no closer to an answer. Choking on an unexpected sob she breathed deep of that elusive scent that teased her mercilessly. She growled, satisfied when the sound broke over her self-pitying sobs with greater volume.

She was tired of feeling sorry for herself. Tired of worrying. So Nikolai wanted to play rough with her? So be it. Rough is how the game would be. A compulsion overcame her, forgotten until just that moment. But now was just as good a time as any to recall her meeting with Adrian Darkwood, she supposed. She had some questions that needed answering. Now.

Chapter Sixteen

ഗ

"Mr. Darkwood will see you now, Ms. Thurman."

Julia thanked the receptionist and went to the door that separated Adrian Darkwood's office from the lobby of The Living Forest's headquarters. The conservation group had been a cornerstone of wildlife and forestry conservation for the past forty years—even Julia, who was decidedly not in the know about such ventures, had heard of their great accomplishments, and not only through playing hostess at their parties. The Living Forest conservation group and its representatives were often in the news, working on saving as much of the Earth and its creatures as they could, preserving them for future generations.

Opening the door, Julia was struck anew with that strange feeling of compulsion—as if her actions were not by her choice alone—and entered with a mixed feeling of anticipation and dread.

Adrian Darkwood was seated behind a large, ornate oaken desk, decorated with an unmistakably Native American design. Buffalo and Elk were carved in various stages of flight over great plains, being chased by warriors on horseback and on foot with their hunting dogs. It was a grand piece of art and immensely pleased Julia's discerning eye.

"Where did you find your desk? I love the inlaid carvings. It must have taken the artist forever to capture the scenes just so."

"Alas, my appeal dims before that of my desk," he said with a warm smile, obviously not at all displeased with her reaction. "Actually, my father carved the piece in honor of my coming to work here ten years ago. He will be pleased to hear your comments on it, for you yourself are an artist. Are you not?"

Julia tore her eyes away from the desk, surprised that he knew that about her. "Yes, I am," she said proudly. "But how would you know that?"

"I have seen some of your work at your school, in the gallery."

"Really?" She was shocked that he even had knowledge of what school she attended. How odd. "I hope you liked what you saw, though I can tell you now that I've since done better."

"A true artist never stops learning their craft. And yes, I very much liked what I saw. You have true talent, Julia. A rare and wonderful gift."

"Thank you." She was growing more and more used to not blushing and stammering in the midst of such conversation. She squared her shoulders and continued, noting an old, age worn book before Adrian on the desk out of the corner of her eye. "But I didn't come here to discuss my artwork, pleasant though it may be for my ego."

Adrian laughed, throwing back his handsome head and flashing brilliant white teeth. "Of course you didn't." His chuckles subsided. "Are you hungry, Julia? I find that I am famished."

With some surprise Julia noted that she was indeed hungry, even though she'd only just eaten some peanut butter on crackers before she'd left her apartment.

But Adrian didn't give her time to nod her assent before he rose from his seat. He grabbed the book before him and walked around the desk to her side. "Why don't we go down the street to the bistro and grab a bite to eat? My treat. I find that serious conversation flows best over a good hearty meal." He offered her his arm in a gallant gesture.

Julia smiled and accepted his offering and together they exited the building in search of food.

Unnoticed, their watcher followed at a safe distance.

* * * * *

"So why have you sought me out, Julia Thurman?" Adrian asked as he helped to seat her at the table.

Julia gave it some thought, then said firmly and without shame, "To be honest, I have no real idea why I came today. I just felt that I had to, you see, that I had to speak to you. Does that make any sense to you, because it really doesn't make much sense to me."

"Perhaps you have questions for me?" he urged.

"What answers could you possibly give me? You have no idea what is going on in my life right now, believe me."

"You'll tell me if I guess right in saying that these questions involve our Mr. Nikolai Tamits, won't you?" His dark chocolate eyes were wise beyond their years, all knowing and powerful in their knowledge.

"Why should I admit any such thing to you? I don't know you."

"But I can assure you that I know you, Julia. I have made it a point to learn everything I can about you."

"Why on earth would you do that?" Julia asked in surprise.

"There are always reasons for what I do, Julia, have no doubts about that. And I promise you that my interest in you and your missing Russian bears no nefarious undertones. I wish you no ill will."

"How did you now that Nikolai is..." She trailed off, uncertain how much to reveal and how much to keep to herself.

It didn't matter. Adrian was obviously well informed. "Missing? That his whereabouts have been unknown for the past four days?" Julia gasped at his accuracy. "I told you. I have made it a point to learn as much about you and Nikolai as I can. It wasn't hard to find out that he has been checked out of his hotel by you, and that he has yet to return home to his kin in Russia."

Julia started at that bit of information. "So he's still here? He hasn't gone back home? Do you know where he is?" Julia growled and clenched her fists in her lap to restrain herself from reaching over the table for Adrian's lapels—the better to shake the information out of him—and took a deep, steadying breath.

"Please calm yourself, Julia. I do not know where Nikolai is at this time." His dark eyes scanned the area, as if expecting to find the answers to her question amongst the mill of the crowded restaurant, before coming to rest on her once more. "And I only know that he hasn't returned home because I have spoken to his cousin-by-marriage, Brianna Basileus, who is also our company CEO. She told me only just this morning that she has had no word from him since he left your apartment four days ago."

"So she's spoken to him? What did he say? Is he all right?"

"Her husband, Ivan, spoke to him. I don't know the details of the conversation. I'm sorry."

Julia's heart fell. Now she had more questions than ever before. If Nikolai hadn't returned home then where was he? Why didn't he come to her? Was he safe, or had the change taken him and placed him in danger?

"I don't understand what's going on anymore. I'm so confused about...everything," she admitted, slouching in her seat with a weary moan.

"There is nothing you can do but worry for now, Julia, so I suggest you let it go. For now, there is much to discuss between just the two of us without worries of Nikolai and his whereabouts. There is much for you to learn, about yourself, I have no doubt. You are changing, Julia, in many ways. I can see it. Those around us can sense it, though they don't understand it. You need your answers and will hear as many as I can give you, I promise you that. But first, let us order our meal. Ah, yes, here comes our waiter." Adrian sent her a comforting wink and a smile as he motioned for their server to approach.

Strangely enough she did feel comforted around Adrian Darkwood, despite all of his cryptic words. He was an unusual man, a beautiful man—though she only noted this truth with her artist's eye and not her libido—but he was also non-threatening. Julia suspected that he could be quite threatening and dangerous indeed if the opportunity arose, but for now he was only a kind individual, offering her the comfort of his company. He seemed an enigma to her, at the same time both gentle and volatile in emotion and demeanor. How odd that she should notice such a thing, she who had never been able to size up a member of the opposite sex with much success in her entire life.

"Shall I order for the both of us, Julia?" he asked politely, breaking over her thoughts with his melodious voice.

"Sure, it's your dime," she lightly responded with an unsteady smile.

"Well then, sir," Adrian addressed their host. "I'd like to order two sirloins. Extra, extra rare."

Chapter Seventeen

ꟸ

Julia ate with voracious appetite, devouring her nearly raw steak, she who had never enjoyed a steak without it being burnt to a crisp. And for once in her life she didn't slather steak sauce over the meat, preferring to leave the flavor and texture of the juicy cut of beef untouched. How strange.

How delicious! She was surprised to note that she could almost eat another, so heady was her appetite today.

"So basically what I'm saying is this. You've been envenomed by an alpha werewolf, my dear."

Julia was startled out of her quiet enjoyment of her meal. She hadn't heard a word Adrian had said for at least the past ten minutes! She'd been enraptured by the filling perfection of her steak. What had he said?

"Could you repeat that last bit, Adrian. I could have sworn you said..." she faltered.

"You've been envenomed by an alpha werewolf. By Nikolai. It's only a matter of time now."

"I'm...I'm sorry. What do you mean? How did you know that Nikolai is a..."

"You haven't been listening to me, have you?" Adrian admonished.

"It's just...I was so hungry. And the steak was so good. I don't normally eat steak rare like this. In fact, I-I never have." Julia felt her stomach contract with fear and her hoarsely spoken words faltered over and over with her nervousness. "What...w-what did you say?"

"Nikolai is from a race of wolf-people, a werewolf for lack of a better term. But you knew that, didn't you?"

"Yes," she admitted in a whisper. "How in the world did you know that?"

"I have spent my entire life studying tribes such as his."

"But he said his was the only pack."

"He is misinformed. But that is not his fault. Most of his kind live in secrecy and never learn of others outside their own families. Nikolai himself was raised in a remote location, far from the opportunity to encounter others like himself. His tribe is much removed, having lived high in their mountain range for centuries, never feeling the need to venture far beyond their borders. It isn't surprising that he would be unaware of the repercussions a mating between himself—an alpha—and a human."

"What...repercussions?"

"You weren't listening to me at all." Adrian chuckled, but it was a mirthless sound. "You will be shocked at first, but that's to be expected. You have mated with an alpha male of a strong werewolf tribe. He has bitten you, has he not? I can sense that he has."

"Y-yes...he bit me. But it wasn't bad, just a nip." She felt the need to defend Nikolai's loss of control.

"But his teeth broke through your skin. Did he draw blood?"

"A little," she admitted.

"Then you have been envenomed by the poison in the glands that rest behind Nikolai's fangs. He injected that poison—or hormone, or enzyme, whatever you want to call it—into your blood stream when he broke through your flesh. He was probably quite wild to bite you before it happened, feverish and irritable, but afterwards he was calmer...wasn't he?"

"Y...y-yes." Oh god, how could this be? Was it a dream? Had she truly lost her mind?

"It is his instinct to claim you, to join you to him and make you like he is. Though I doubt that he realizes it. I suspect he left you because he was afraid he might harm you somehow, especially after biting you."

"How can you know all of this? I don't understand how you can have all these answers, when Nikolai doesn't have them himself."

"It is because I come from a similar ilk as Nikolai. I, too, am a werewolf—or skinwalker as many of my people would say—and I knew from the beginning that Nikolai was one of us, when I first shook his hand. Do not be alarmed!" He reached for her hand across the table when she gasped at the unexpected news. "There are many of us, more than you could ever guess, I would wager. But it is not so frightening a thing as you might expect," he said in an effort to soothe her.

"I don't believe you," she said in an unsteady voice, knowing already in the back of her mind that he spoke the truth.

Adrian flashed her another toothy grin, this time revealing a set of sharp, elongated fangs. "You have no idea how difficult this is to do in public," he muttered. "I can only affect so much of my change at will without losing control and braying like a hound at the moon." He laughed at himself, but it was a dark and guttural sound, coming from such a sharp-toothed mouth.

"Okay. I believe you. Put those away, please," she beseeched before continuing in a weak voice. "If you could tell what he was just by shaking his hand, how come Nikolai didn't know you were a...," she looked around nervously and lowered her words, "a *werewolf*?"

"Nikolai is not so informed as I, I told you. I know what signs to look for, what nuances make another werewolf stand out in a crowd. Nikolai does not. He sensed a threat in me, instinctively, though he could not pinpoint what that threat was. He sensed the alpha strain in me, that strength of will and purpose that makes me a natural leader among my own kind. It was why he became agitated when I spoke to you at the party, if you'll remember his reaction. It is why he is naturally cautious around me…just as I am cautious around him. I would not want to engage in a supremacy fight with your Nikolai, I have my doubts about who the victor would be."

"And you're saying that I am…becoming like him?"

"Yes. Very much so. Already your appetites have changed, you crave rare and nearly uncooked meats, and you have a natural inclination to be territorial when it comes to discussions concerning Nikolai. You miss him, with an inexplicable yearning I have no doubt, as you are true mates. You hold yourself with a grace—a poise—that you did not possess but a few nights ago at the party in the hotel, that is plain for me to see. Your eyes are brighter, not yet burning as Nikolai's often do, but far from human now just the same. You have a draw on humans, male and female, that you haven't even noticed yet. There are eyes watching you right now, enraptured by your animal magnetism. You may not experience a full change with the moon for several more months…but already it has begun. You are no longer human, Julia."

"Oh my god. How can this be? What am I going to do now?"

"The only thing that you can do. You will find Nikolai and you will give him this." Adrian reached out and handed her the old book she had noticed on his desk earlier.

"What is that?" she asked, throat gone dry and aching. So much had happened to her in the past week. She wasn't sure how to react.

"It is a memoir, written by Alexi Balovski, Brianna's late uncle. It is an account of the many werewolf packs he met with on his travels throughout the world. In it, Nikolai will find all the answers to all the questions he may have regarding you, your change, and the mating bond between the two of you. There have been other such marriages between werewolf and human—I myself am a product of such a union."

"Then Brianna is a werewolf, too? How can that be, without Nikolai's knowledge?"

"She is not a werewolf, Julia. Her mate is not an alpha and therefore cannot possess the venom necessary to infect his mate with the genetic material that instigates the change. As far as I am aware, only the strongest of alpha males—a born leader—can change his mate into a werewolf. I suspect it is an evolutionary maneuver intended to keep the stronger bloodlines pure within the race."

"You say you are a product of a werewolf and a human…how did your mother react to her change?" Julia was almost too afraid to ask.

"At first she was angry with my father for changing her. In fact, she didn't speak to him for nearly nine months—the entire time she was pregnant with me. But she didn't change fully into her wolf form for almost two years so she had time to grow accustomed to the idea. I don't know how long it will be before you change, it is different from person to person or so I've heard. But my mother was never in any danger. My father eased her into the life of a werewolf with gentle patience. She once told me that had she the choice to do it all over again she would have made my father envenom her sooner in their courtship." He laughed, obviously pleased by the memory. "I don't think you should worry overmuch. I know you will be frightened at first, but I have a feeling you will make an excellent alpha female in Nikolai's pack. But first you must find him."

"How? I have no idea where he could be. He hasn't called me or come by the hotel. And if his family has no idea where he is, I'm out of ideas."

"Your lupine senses are awakening, and if I'm not mistaken, the sense of smell is the first to be magnified in a human. Do you think perhaps you can hunt him by scent? Cast your face to the wind and see if you can separate his signature smell from those around you. I assure you, that if he is still in the city—and I am certain that he would not stray far from your side—you will be able to track him."

"I…I've smelled him on more than one occasion the past few days. But I was sure it was just my imagination," she whispered. Dare she hope? Dare she give such a wild idea—*hunting* him for goodness sake—a try?

Why not? She was out of options. If what Adrian said was true and she was changing into a werewolf, she needed to find Nikolai. Sooner rather than later.

"If you are able to lock onto his scent, it will lead you to him."

Julia sat, trembling in her seat, thinking. It was a long time before she spoke, but when she did it was full of conviction. She had come to a decision. She would stick by it.

"Tell me what I must do."

* * * * *

Julia meandered about the grounds of the park, wondering if she hadn't completely lost her mind. She raised her head to the wind, keeping in mind the crash course in tracking that Adrian had given her before they had parted company a little over an hour ago, and caught a faint whiff of Nikolai's elusive scent. Where he had seemed to be in front of her but a moment ago, he now seemed to be behind her. It was enough to drive her crazy, this expedition into the park. Alone.

At twilight. Searching for a man who quite probably would be really unhappy to find her here.

Grrr, she had no idea what she was doing!

Julia was pulled forcibly from her thoughts when an arm came and wrapped itself around her neck. A menacing voice grated into her ear.

"One sound and I'll cut your throat, girlie."

Great, this was all she needed. Strangely enough she felt no fear, only aggravation, so her words were perhaps a little more flippant than they should have been under the circumstances. "Give me a break mister. I have no money for you to steal so why don't you just go find something else to amuse yourself with, hmm?"

"If you don't have money, perhaps you have something else of value that I can take." He laughed and Julia almost gagged as the fetid smell of him washed over her. She knew instinctively that she didn't smell his physical scent so much as his emotional one. He was a truly disgusting piece of filth, her attacker.

Perhaps it wasn't wise to tell him, but she did, in lurid detail.

Another man stepped from out of the shadows and trees just ahead of her with a smirk. "Oooh, I like 'em feisty. How 'bout you, Davey?"

"Oh yeah, you know I do," said the man at her ear. He released a vulgar sound of vile enjoyment and sloppily licked at her neck and ear.

Julia shuddered in disgust and pulled free from her attacker with surprisingly little effort on her part. "Back off, guys. I'm not in the mood for it," she growled out, stepping back several paces into the camouflage of the trees.

"What a little Amazon you are. I'm going to really enjoy this." The man who had held her rushed at her suddenly, clearly intent on running her to the ground.

Julia saw the scene unfold with an odd sense of calm. It was as though the two men moved now in slow motion, allowing her to time her movements to theirs with little effort. The first thug came upon her like a rampaging bull, knife arm raised in a threatening manner. Julia merely struck out at his arm, seeing her movements as though they were exponentially faster than those of her attacker. There was a crack as her hand struck his arm and quick as a flash the man was on the ground, cradling his arm and crying like a baby. White bone protruded from a bloody gash in his arm—she had fractured it with nothing but a casual swipe of her hand.

Oh lord…what had she done? She'd never hurt another person intentionally before and certainly not to such a severe degree.

"Goodness! I'm so sorry. Are you ok?" she asked, clumsily moving to his side in her distress.

But the other man, her second would-be attacker, had no such concerns for his partner. He came upon her and in her preoccupation he managed to strike her a blow to the head with his booted foot. Julia fell like a stone, feeling as though a thousand shards of glass had exploded in her brain. She howled out in pain, a wild, animalistic sound that would have frightened her and her attacker both, had they not been locked in combat.

The man came down on top of her, striking blows to her face and ribs with a look of fierce satisfaction and glee on his face. Julia, dazed from the blows, did the only thing she could while shielding her face from further damage, and struck out with her feet. Her attacker went flying into the air like a rag doll, landing several feet away from her, sputtering with his own pain and rage.

The man stumbled unsteadily to his feet after several moments and looked at her with an expression of horror. "What the hell are you, lady?"

Julia was too far gone in her pain to answer him. She only had thoughts of getting away, far away, and licking her wounds…both figuratively and literally. She wondered how she could get away without him catching up to her, bruised and battered as she was. But she needn't have worried—the man forgot all about her in the next instant.

A roar split through the clearing, loud enough to be heard throughout the corners of the city that lay beyond the park's borders. It was a sound of pure, unadulterated rage, the likes of which few humans had ever encountered. Julia looked up to see a large, dark form somersault through the air, coming to land lightly in front of her in a protective crouch. Her attacker screamed loud and shrill upon looking into the face of her savior, obviously getting the fright of his life. He turned to take flight, leaving his partner in crime still lying in agony on the ground behind him.

Julia's savior leapt high, somersaulted twice in the air, and landed squarely in front of the fleeing man. The light of the risen moon caught his face and glinted off his ice blue eyes and brilliant white fangs, revealing his fierce, wild beauty.

"Nikolai!" Had there ever been a doubt in her mind that it was he? All her worries and fears fled as if they had never been. Her mate would take care of her now…there was nothing more for her to fret about. She knew instinctively that all would be well.

Nikolai paid her little heed, intent only on the man who had dared to raise a hand to harm his mate. He bared his fangs in another fierce roar and lunged at the criminal, sinking his teeth deep into his throat. Julia cried out at the sight and stumbled to her feet, rushing on unsteady legs to his side.

"Stop it, Nikolai, you'll kill him!"

Her mate only growled around his mouthful of flesh and sinew, and burrowed his jaws deeper into his prey.

"Please, Nikolai. Don't do this, it's not worth it. Let him go."

Nikolai jerked away, revealing that he had yet to break the skin of the man's throat. "He hurt you! How can you defend him?"

"I'm not defending him, I'm defending you. You don't want to have his blood on your hands, Nikolai. I know that you don't. After all these years of hating yourself for killing those hunters that attacked your brothers, do you think you have it in you to take another life in anger like this?"

"How could you know about that?" he asked in a shocked cry.

"You told me about it, back at my apartment when you were rambling. You told me how those poachers hunted your brothers for their fur, how you chased after them and barely managed to save them, how your brother Jarus sustained grave injuries to his leg from one of the trap the hunters had set. You killed those men to protect your brothers—you had no other choice—and you've hated yourself for it. But now you do have a choice. You don't have to kill this man for hurting me. You've scared him senseless...let that be enough. Let him go."

Nikolai was unearthly still for several endless moments, clearly weighing her words in his mind. It seemed hours had passed before he stirred, and full night was upon them. The man beneath Nikolai was beyond them, having passed out during the attack, and Julia was grateful for that much at least. One wrong move from the man could have triggered Nikolai's deadly instincts and perhaps cost him his life.

"You are right, love. You are right," he murmured and rose from his crouch over the fallen man. "Are you terribly injured? Do you need a doctor?"

"No, I'm fine. Just a little bruised, but other than that I'll be okay. How about you? Are you all right? I haven't heard anything from you...I've been so worried."

"I am sorry. I have never been far from you, love. But I cannot trust myself around you. I left you to protect you from me."

Julia led him away from the two fallen attackers, deep into the wooded area of the park. She wanted as much distance between them and the men as possible, in case Nikolai changed his mind and decided to finish what he had started. He was about to get a blast of her temper and she didn't want to see how he would react with those vermin near at hand to take out his aggression on.

When they were a safe distance away Julia turned and let him have it. "Just who the hell do you think you are, leaving me hanging like that? I thought something terrible had happened to you, that you were in danger, or at the very least unstable because of your change. And here you are, fit as a fiddle and acting as if you did the most noble thing you could think of by leaving me!"

Nikolai flinched at the volume of her voice, which was indeed loud—had he but known it, her voice was louder now than any human's could have been—and raised his hands in a gesture of supplication and surrender. "Please forgive me, Julia. I did what I thought was right at the time. I knew that you would be hurt, I will not lie, but I promise you that it is nothing compared to the pain you would have felt had I lost control. I was afraid I would kill you. I had to leave."

"But you didn't leave. As you said, you've been near me all along. What difference does it make if you are with me openly or in secret? You're still around me just the same."

"I know. I am ashamed to admit that I could not leave you completely. But at least this way there is some distance between us, allowing you some safety should I become more beast than man."

"Tell me something. Do you feel bestial around me now?"

"Well…no, actually. I do not." He seemed surprised to realize it.

"Have you felt agitated at all since that day when you bit me? Even the least bit out of control?"

"No," he murmured with a frown.

"Don't you wonder why that is?"

"I admit that I have not given it much thought until now. I have been too busy following you, seeing to your safety." His eyes blazed fiercely as he continued. "And that reminds me. How do you think it made me feel to see you strolling off today with Adrian Darkwood? Did you not for one instant think how that might hurt my feelings should I discover it?" His voice was rising, growing more and more angry by the second.

"Adrian Darkwood and I met as friends. And you should be glad we did, too. He's the one who told me how I could find you. Here, he gave me this to give to you." Julia reached into her purse, which luckily enough she had managed to keep on her person during the tussle with the muggers, and pulled out the book Adrian had given her.

"What is it?"

"It's a book, a diary of sorts, written by Brianna's uncle. It has a lot of information about werewolves in it—real werewolves—that he encountered during the travels of his life. You were mistaken in thinking yours was the only werewolf pack, Nikolai. According to this man, there are hundreds more like yours."

"But how can this be?" he breathed in wonder, taking the book from her with unsteady hands.

"There's something else you should know, Nikolai." She wasn't sure how to break the news to him so she rushed headlong into the explanation as best she could. "I am turning into a werewolf. That bite you gave me...it's done something to me. Adrian says you've infected me with...werewolfitis." She laughed at herself, thought it was a weak sound at best.

"Adrian knows of this? You told him?"

"Don't get all bent out of shape," she said in exasperation. "He told me actually. He knew just from meeting you that you were a werewolf, and he knew that we were mates that night at the party. He knew that this would happen between us, and tried to help me understand it a little."

"How could he know so much about this?"

"Because he's a werewolf, too. And he's spent his whole life learning from Brianna's uncle about other werewolf packs throughout the world. The Living Forest group is comprised of people like him, studying ancient forests and the creatures within. Werewolves, wereleopards, and goodness knows how many other shape shifting species. There are countless others like you, living in seclusion in the forests and rainforests of the world. Adrian says it's all there, in that book, if you care to read through it."

"I cannot believe it. It is as if everything has changed in my view of the world. And you...you say you are changing? Becoming like me. I do not know what to say."

"Say you'll love me, no matter how furry I may get when the moon is full. Just as I love you." There, she had said it. It hadn't been so hard after all.

"Julia...you will always have my heart. And if you are going to be a Bodark like me, I will be happier than I can admit in words. There is so much that I can share with you as a wolf. So much I can teach you...show to you. I dare not believe such a miraculous thing is possible."

"Believe it. You have to. I'm already changing. I broke that guy's arm back there and all I did was swat it away. I'm stronger, that's for certain. And I can hear things better, smell better. In fact, I tracked you by scent all the way out here."

"I led you here. I was angry about your meeting with Adrian. I wanted to confront you…ask you if you still cared for me. Perhaps find a way to be with you. If only for a little while."

"We can be together forever, Nikolai. That is, if you're all right with that." She couldn't help but feel a little uneasy. She'd never professed undying love to another person before tonight.

"What about your school? And your life here?"

"I have no life here without you. And school doesn't matter to me so much as it did before I met you. In fact, since you bit me, I've been doing some pretty incredible work. I think I've reached a new height in my potential. I'm thinking about hiring an agent and making a name for myself on the open market."

"Would you live with me, in my homeland? I would live here if you asked it of me, but I must admit that I do not like it here."

Julia laughed, feeling all of her uncertainties leave as if they had never been. "I don't like it much here, either. I'd love to live with you, Nikolai. You'll have to teach me Russian, of course, so I can blend in with the natives." She laughed again.

"There is much that I wish to teach you…Russian being the least of them." His eyes burned with a sudden fire.

"Hey, don't look at me like that. We're miles from home, so don't tease. My libido can't take that look just now."

"What does the location of your home have to do with anything?" he leered comically.

Julia laughed, but felt a thrill to her toes when he lunged playfully for her. She managed to dodge him, once, twice, and then turned on her heels to run, laughing all the way. Behind her, Nikolai gave a mock howl and sprinted after her. For half an hour they chased each other around the park, playfully tussling when they caught up with one another, growling and yipping like young cubs. Then, breathless, they collapsed in a copse of young trees, looking up at the sky as they held each other and calmed.

"The moon is bright tonight. It will be full in less than a fortnight."

"Yes," Julia breathed, entranced by the pull of it in the night sky.

"Are you scared of what might happen?"

"A little. A lot. I don't know." She laughed at her own indecisiveness. "Are you scared?"

"No. I am more excited than anything."

Julia couldn't resist, she laid her hand coyly on his groin, unsurprised to find it hard and heavy beneath her palm. "How excited?"

"This excited..." He growled and rolled over her, nuzzling his face into the valley of her breasts. Seconds later it seemed, they were both nude, and Julia had no recollection of how she had gotten that way.

"You work fast." She laughed.

"I cannot have my prey escaping now can I?" he teased back.

There was no more room for talk as Nikolai lowered his mouth to hers. His lips were as soft as she remembered them being. His tongue slipped past her lips and dueled with hers, filling her mouth with the wild taste of him. While he kissed her, his fingers stroked from Julia's neck to her knees. He caressed her breasts, belly, navel and mons with infinite care. He pinched one of her nipples, lightly rolling it between his thumb and forefinger, until she cried out and arched up against him, seeking more of the delicious torment.

His hand roved down, down between her thighs. She spread them wide, eagerly, and his weight settled easily between them. His fingertips dipped into her wet heat, rubbing lightly over her labia and clitoris, knowing just how to tease and torment her into wanting more, more and still more. Her hips bucked up against his hand, aching for a firmer touch, a deeper penetration. He eagerly obliged her, pressing two of his long fingers deep into her channel, stretching her, preparing her for him. His eyes blazed down into hers, keeping them locked together, as he brought his hand up to show her the glistening evidence of her own arousal. With a breathless moan she watched as he licked her juices from his fingers, obviously savoring the taste of her.

He released his fingers with a wet, suctioning sound, and placed them once more at her vagina. This time it was three fingers that entered her body. Julia cried out and bucked against his hand, and he began a rhythmic thrusting in and out of her burning pussy, making her wild with need. His mouth roved down to her nipple, drawing it tightly into his wet, hot mouth. His lips, teeth and tongue worked her, driving her crazy with lust and arousal. Her body felt swollen, achy and hungry for everything he had to give.

"Please, please," she moaned over and over again, thrashing her head about on the ground, heedless to the debris that caught in her hair as she did so.

"Please what, Julia. Tell me what you want," he urged her, murmuring the words against her hard, swollen nipple.

"I want...I want..."

"Tell me."

"I want it all," she cried, bucking up against his hand, forcing his fingers deeper into her welcoming body.

"Then you shall have it," he promised in a dark voice. He pulled his fingers free from her and rubbed her wetness over the tip of his cock. He wrapped his fist around the base and pumped himself with his hand. He positioned the crown of his sex at her portal and in one great lunge, thrust into the heart of her.

Julia screamed at the sudden invasion, both in pleasure, surprise and pain. Nikolai raised her hips up, wrapping her legs around his waist and began to thrust into her. She felt a gentle probing at the flesh of her anus then gasped anew when Nikolai's thumb entered her there. Her body felt split open, wide and receptive to his whim. Nerve endings she'd never even known she had awoke where Nikolai's thumb carefully pistoned, and she clamped down on him with ecstatic pleasure. Julia clearly heard the wet and greedy noises her pussy made as he thrust in and out of her, and the sounds aroused her to a fevered pitch. She rose up and kissed him, stabbing her tongue into his mouth as his cock and thumb stabbed into her lower orifices.

A moment later she howled into his mouth and came with a sweet, warm rush of liquid between her legs, easing his way further as he rocked inside of her. Nikolai shuddered and pounded into her with a fierce rhythm, shaking her very bones with the force of his thrusts. He roared his satisfaction to the heavens, even as her body still pulsed with its own release, and filled her with the cream of his climax. Over and over his body poured itself into hers until her womb was flooded to bursting with his come. Then, when it seemed she would burst with him, Nikolai collapsed onto her, taking her nipple into his mouth once again as he calmed.

It was almost dawn when they rose from their lover's bower, dressed and headed for home. Hand in hand they walked, ready to face the day ahead. Together.

Epilogue

ꟃ

Brianna closed her uncle's memoirs with a happy sigh. "I can't believe he knew all about your kind, Ivan."

"He was a smart man, your uncle Alexi."

"How on earth could he have suspected that I would find you here? It's amazing—he actually discovered the existence of your pack when he was a young boy, studied you from afar without your knowledge…and he never told anyone—he devoted his whole life to finding others like you and preserving your habitats. It's as though I never really knew my uncle at all. He had a secret life I knew nothing about."

"Does it say in there why he never contacted us? Why he never came forward and introduced himself?"

"He just mentions that he had other plans regarding your family. And you know what else? He sent me here on purpose—his deathbed wish was more than just a whim—he hoped that I would stumble on your village and perhaps discover the same passion for conservation as he had…and the wonder of it all is that I actually did."

"I for one am incredibly grateful to your uncle. Without him we may never have met." Ivan growled after the words, as if in protest over so dire a thought.

"Oh I wouldn't go that far. I think we were destined to meet, you and I. But perhaps we wouldn't have found each other so soon. I'm glad Alexi sent me here. Very glad."

"Well, are you ready to go down to the village proper and witness the pack's change?"

"Ready as I'll ever be. You know, I'm never going to get used to this. It's all still so magical for me," Brianna said with a smile.

"So you've no regrets in coming to stay here with us?"

"None. You know that, you big goob." She laughed.

"And how do you feel about having another human come and stay with us?"

"Julia's not so human anymore. But I like her very much. I think she's a perfect mate for Nikolai. She'll keep him on his toes. And keep him from being so serious about protecting the pack all the time."

"My thoughts exactly, love." Ivan leaned down and kissed her lips. "I'm glad that things finally worked out between them."

"Shall we walk down together?

"I'll never leave your side."

* * * * *

"According to Adrian your change will probably not be for another few months yet, even though you are far along in the metamorphosis."

"Good. I doubt I'm ready. I haven't even seen you change yet, Nikolai, not fully. I have no idea what to expect." Julia shuffled her feet, looking around her at all the other werewolves, men, women and their families gathered around them as they awaited the rise of the full moon in the sky.

"Do not be nervous, love. I promise that no harm will befall you so long as I am near you."

"I love you Nikolai."

"I love you too, fair Julia. Now, enough of this serious talk. This is a night of celebration!" His last words were loud, for the benefit of the others around them. "We will hunt tonight and run the wilds until morning, under the wondrous light of the *mooooooooon*." He threw back his head and howled. Each of his pack mates followed suit until a symphony of wolfish cries rose up towards the heavens.

Nikolai looked down at Julia again. "Are you sure you are up to this?"

"Absolutely. I don't want to miss out on one minute of it. Just remember not to make any sudden moves towards me when you're a wolf." She laughed at her own nervous words.

"I promise to try. I am not completely myself in that form, but I will have enough of my wits about me to recognize my mate…or so Ivan tells me." He laughed. "I am a novice at this myself."

"And what if I do change?"

"Then you and I will have to find a quiet corner in which to explore your new form…which I am sure will be just as sexy as your present one." He flashed her a wicked, lascivious grin.

"You beast." She shivered with desire at the hungry look in his eye. Her hormones had been out of control during the past couple of weeks, ever since Nikolai had bitten her. She wanted sex several times a day now. Luckily, Nikolai was more than happy to oblige her whenever she had need of him.

"I may be a beast, but I am *your* beast, love." He leaned down and nuzzled her ear playfully.

"And don't you forget it."

There was a stirring in the crowd of people. "The moon is on the rise, Julia," Nikolai whispered, his voice full of awe and anticipation.

Julia stood next to Nikolai as it happened—his change. It was a magical moment when his body shifted, blurred and reformed. The transformation only took a few short moments and then, all around her, stood giant wolves shuffling their feet and moving to flank their leader. Nikolai was beautiful beyond words. Standing on his great pawed feet he reached nearly to her waist in height, his thick golden pelt shining in the silvery light of the moon. Black marks of kohl rimmed his eyes as they did when he was a man, giving him an exotic look.

She felt a tingling and looked down at her own body, gasping to find her body covered in a light pelt of yellow fur. "Oh lord look at me," she wailed.

Nikolai the wolf moved over to her, sniffed her once and then yipped at her. He seemed to be smiling up at her, sharp teeth flashing like white diamonds in the dusk twilight. He seemed to be reassuring her that she was just as beautiful to him now as she had been but moments ago. Surprisingly enough, Julia felt some measure of acceptance take over her worries and she shrugged her shoulders with a little laugh.

"Well, shall we go, love?" she asked, nearly jumping when she heard how deep and gravelly her voice had become. Then she noticed her elongated fangs and yelped, raising her hands up to feel them.

Nikolai nudged her with his great body, rubbing his head against her stomach, and then moved forward, herding her along with him. Instinctively Julia knew this was the moment she had both dreaded and anticipated by turns. The wolves around her knew it too and gave a great howl.

The family of wolves exploded in a flurry of movement, running off into the dark heart of the great forest. Their large golden alpha led them on their hunt.

His mate was beside him every step of the way.

Why an electronic book?

We live in the Information Age—an exciting time in the history of human civilization, in which technology rules supreme and continues to progress in leaps and bounds every minute of every day. For a multitude of reasons, more and more avid literary fans are opting to purchase e-books instead of paper books. The question from those not yet initiated into the world of electronic reading is simply: *Why?*

1. ***Price.*** An electronic title at Ellora's Cave Publishing and Cerridwen Press runs anywhere from 40% to 75% less than the cover price of the exact same title in paperback format. Why? Basic mathematics and cost. It is less expensive to publish an e-book (no paper and printing, no warehousing and shipping) than it is to publish a paperback, so the savings are passed along to the consumer.
2. ***Space.*** Running out of room in your house for your books? That is one worry you will never have with electronic books. For a low one-time cost, you can purchase a handheld device specifically designed for e-reading. Many e-readers have large, convenient screens for viewing. Better yet, hundreds of titles can be stored within your new library—on a single microchip. There are a variety of e-readers from different manufacturers. You can also read e-books on your PC or laptop computer. (Please note that Ellora's Cave does not endorse any specific brands.

You can check our websites at www.ellorascave.com or www.cerridwenpress.com for information we make available to new consumers.)

3. ***Mobility***. Because your new e-library consists of only a microchip within a small, easily transportable e-reader, your entire cache of books can be taken with you wherever you go.
4. ***Personal Viewing Preferences.*** Are the words you are currently reading too small? Too large? Too... *ANNOYING*? Paperback books cannot be modified according to personal preferences, but e-books can.
5. ***Instant Gratification.*** Is it the middle of the night and all the bookstores near you are closed? Are you tired of waiting days, sometimes weeks, for bookstores to ship the novels you bought? Ellora's Cave Publishing sells instantaneous downloads twenty-four hours a day, seven days a week, every day of the year. Our webstore is never closed. Our e-book delivery system is 100% automated, meaning your order is filled as soon as you pay for it.

Those are a few of the top reasons why electronic books are replacing paperbacks for many avid readers.

As always, Ellora's Cave and Cerridwen Press welcome your questions and comments. We invite you to email us at Comments@ellorascave.com or write to us directly at Ellora's Cave Publishing Inc., 1056 Home Avenue, Akron, OH 44310-3502.

ELLORA'S CAVE
ROMANTICA PUBLISHING